THE TOURNAMENT

John Clarke's books include *The Even More Complete Book of Australian Verse* and *A Dagg at My Table*. He recently helped organize the highly successful Sydney Olympic Games.

THE TOURNAMENT

JOHN CLARKE

NEW YORK

First published in Australia by The Text Publishing Company.

 Printed in the United States of America. For information address Hyperion, 77 West 66th Street, New York, New York 10023-6298.

Library of Congress Cataloging-in-Publication Data

Clarke, John, 1948–
The tournament / John Clarke.
p. cm.
ISBN 1-4013-0092-8
1. Tennis—Tournaments—Fiction. 2. Intellectuals—Fiction. I. Title.
PR9619.3.C539T68 2003
823'.914—dc21

2003050869

Hyperion books are available for special promotions and premiums. For details contact Michael Rentas, Manager, Inventory and Premium Sales, Hyperion, 77 West 66th Street, 11th floor, New York, New York 10023, or call 212-456-0133.

FIRST U.S. EDITION

10 9 8 7 6 5 4 3 2 1

for
Charlie Boy

Preliminaries

Day 1

Ibsen and Monet v. James and Twain

If the players in this city aren't careful they're going to be among the most famous people on earth. Paris has gone crazy. More people in the streets would be hard to imagine, and that's not counting the celebrities, the journalists, the experts. Every hotel is booked out. There are flags and banners everywhere, every color under the sun.

Out at the stadium the crowds are already huge as competitors pound the practice courts in preparation for the greatest tournament of the era. Organizers predict it will be the most successful event of its type ever staged. All tickets are sold, there's not a single ground pass left and the worldwide television audience is tipped to be in the billions.

They've opened three more runways at the airport where players and officials have been arriving like migrating birds. Make no mistake about it, this tournament is anyone's and they've come from all corners, the stars of the modern game.

Some have arrived in teams, the Germans last night: Hermann Hesse, Brecht and Weill, Gropius, Carnap and the great Mann, Heidegger, Schweitzer, Ernst. What a lineup!

Reporters tried to get a few words as the players came through but they were hurried out a side door.

"No interviews will be permitted," said a German official.

This morning the Austrians were less formal. Gustav Mahler introduced some of the team: Wittgenstein, Melanie Klein, Werfel, Kokoschka, Gödel and Klimt.

"We're looking forward to playing here," he announced.

"Where is Freud?" asked *Tennis* magazine's Norman Mailer.

"Arriving by train," said Mahler. "Tonight, I think."

From America we have Ernie Hemingway, Fitzgerald, Crosby, Frankie Wright, Ray Chandler, Bix Beiderbecke and Louis Armstrong, Bessie Smith, Gertrude Stein, Isadora Duncan and Mary McCarthy. Amelia Earhart flew her single-seater from New York.

"Great to be here," said Ernie. "The plane was high in the air. I slept and then I ate and drank and then I slept again. The sun came up. I drank again and then I slept. Then the plane banked and came in and landed and stopped and I could hear the great big engines being turned off. That's the way it is."

The South Americans have been training in Italy and turned up yesterday before anybody else: Borges, Rodo, Rivera and Kahlo, Neruda and Villa-Lobos.

The Swiss and the Dutch are here. Watch the Dutch. Their record is excellent and Escher and van Gogh are two of the strongest chances in the men's competition.

The formidable Russian contingent came in over several days. They're taking this seriously and have left nothing to chance: Rachmaninov, Stravinsky, Pavlova, Akhmatova, Eisenstein, Prokofiev, Shostakovich, Pasternak and Chagall, they're all here. And, perhaps most importantly, Chekhov and the Count are in town.

The English hope for glory and are here in numbers. "The strongest team ever to cross the Channel," according to Frank "the Ferret" Leavis, who'll be trying to get through the qualifiers. Lawrence, Waugh, Kipling and Maugham, Auden, Spender and Isherwood are here. Little Bertie Russell and Herbie Wells are here. Edith Sitwell, Dot Sayers, Virginia Stephen-Woolf and Vita Sackville-West are here. Orwell is expected any minute.

From Poland have come the great Nijinsky and Conrad, the gifted Rosa Luxemburg and the fabulous Paderewski. Nijinsky was "pleased to be back. I've always loved playing here. I feel good. Very fit. Watch this." And quite suddenly, wearing an overcoat and carrying three suitcases, he leapt five meters straight up in the air.

Beckett arrived on a bicycle, Joyce and Chaplin by car. Tallulah Bankhead came up the river on a barge. W. C. Fields arrived by dirigible. Buster Keaton was catapulted in from Belgium, Escher arrived through the departure lounge, Dali came by overnight post and Alice Toklas sent herself as an attachment. Einstein said he had come by tram.

"But there is no tram to Paris," corrected George Plimpton from the *Paris Review*.

"That might account for the time lapse," Einstein explained.

And from all over France the French have arrived: Sartre, de Beauvoir, Camus, the considerable Proust, Braque, Derain, Seurat, Debussy, Bernhardt, Cocteau, Satie, Duchamp. What depth there is in the French game! And what will they do in front of their own crowds?

"Where is Picasso?" asked Roland Barthes from *Paris-Match*. "And where is SuperTom?"

But the Spanish champion delayed his arrival at the stadium until late afternoon. Pablo Picasso stepped out of an open sports car to a rapturous reception at 5:55 p.m., just in time to make the evening news.

The London-based American SuperTom Eliot was more subtle, coming in under the radar late at night and staying with friends "to avoid any fuss." His preparation is said to be "perfect, if he gets a decent draw." Opinion seems to be that if he and

Picasso are in opposite halves of the draw we've got a real contest on our hands.

Oscar Wilde is in from London. "Couldn't stay away," he said. "One should always attend events in which one has no possible interest. They are invariably the most rewarding."

"Are you serious?"

"A gentleman should always be serious. It amuses one's butler and fortifies the religious convictions of one's mother."

"But an event which is of no interest cannot possibly be rewarding."

"That is a thesis refuted by its own expression. I'm happy to say that, properly used, the language is full of them."

"But surely if language has meaning, it is because each individual word has meaning. A word that means nothing is useless."

"Everything contains its own opposite. That is its strength. Nothing is itself alone. That is its."

Live television and Internet coverage of this astounding event began with an exhibition doubles match featuring Henrik Ibsen and Claude Monet against Americans Henry James and Mark Twain. The big-hearted Norwegian and the French institution were given a hero's welcome as they came out on Centre Court and memories flooded back as they slipped into their old rhythm. James played a perfectly timed lob at one stage and Ibsen lost sight of the ball. Monet moved away down the service line, keeping the ball over his left shoulder, and prepared to manufacture any kind of a shot to keep the ball in play. At the last minute, going left to give himself room, he hit a backhand crosscourt drive which dropped just over the net.

"I thought it was a forehand down the line," said Twain later. "It looked like a forehand down the line."

"Was it not a forehand down the line?" said James. "My clear recollection is that it was a forehand down the line."

"We are doomed," said Ibsen.

"It was supposed to *look* like a forehand down the line," said Monet.

"It did," said Twain. "How do you do that? That's brilliant."

"I try to make it look as if it *feels* as if it's a forehand down the line," said Monet.

"Try not to be absurd," said James. "Nobody of any importance is persuaded by what something looks as if it feels like."

"Are you kidding, Henry?" said his partner. "Why didn't we get it back?"

Ever the showman, Twain pulled out an armory of trick shots and on several occasions all Monet and Ibsen could do was stand and applaud. Playing in bare feet because there was a frog asleep in one of his shoes, Twain hit the ball through his legs, around his back and from as far as three rows back in the stands.

"He's completely ridiculous to play against," said Ibsen. "He drives you crazy. I spoke to him about it at one stage and he called an official over and told him I didn't have a ticket and he'd never seen me before in his life."

"You need to keep these old guys on their toes," said Twain, "or they'll seize up altogether. I promised Ibbo's wife I'd run him around a bit."

Ibsen was the one player of his era Twain never defeated. "Ibbo was too complicated for me," he said. "I could never get within a day's walk of him. He seemed to understand things the rest of us knew nothing about."

Ibsen made light of this regard. "They're good fellows," he said. "That James is a joy to watch. I just try to get the thing back over the net. With him it's an art. If youngsters want to learn the way the game ought to be played, they should watch Henry."

"Don't watch me," said James. "Look at Monet. He has revolutionized the way it's done in France."

"He's great," said Twain, "although don't tell him we said that. What's French for 'little fat guy'?"

"Twain," said Ibsen, "is a great tactician and a beautiful liar. It is true he never beat me. What he fails to point out is that we never played each other. The first time we won the All of England doubles title together, he played such shots as I've never seen and when we were presented with the trophy he said to me, 'Hey, Whiskers, you're pretty good at this. Have you ever tried fishing?'"

And Monet?

"Dream partner," said Ibsen. "A genius."

In what way?

"In the way geniuses are," replied Ibsen.

But how do you know he's a genius?

"He looks as if he feels like a genius," said Ibsen.

Umpire Rodin, from France, hardly moved.

The World Tennis Organization (WTO) announced the men's and women's seedings at an official lunch. Aside from the removal of a woman named Violet Trefusis following an incident involving a Mars bar, the occasion was said to have gone "very well indeed." The seedings are:

MEN

1 Chekhov, 2 Yeats, 3 Eliot, 4 Einstein, 5 Joyce, 6 Conrad, 7 Picasso, 8 Tolstoy, 9 Pasternak, 10 Duchamp, 11 Paderewski, 12 van Gogh, 13 Freud, 14 Chaplin, 15 Puccini, 16 Nijinsky.

WOMEN

1 Earhart, 2 de Beauvoir, 3 Pavlova, 4 Bernhardt, 5 Pankhurst, 6 Stein, 7 Stephen-Woolf, 8 Garbo, 9 Christie, 10 Chanel, 11 Stopes, 12 Melba, 13 Montessori, 14 Mead, 15 Akhmatova, 16 Pickford.

There are no surprises among the men with world number 1 Tony Chekhov and Big Bill Yeats heading the list, which otherwise proceeds in accordance with current WTO computer rankings.

Why the women's seedings are at odds with international rankings is not clear although some observers say their game is less predictable than the men's.

"I don't think that's the real story," said American Mary McCarthy. "The WTO doesn't know what's going on in women's tennis. How the hell would they? They're not interested."

Suggestions that the seedings of the two French players, Simone de Beauvoir and Sarah Bernhardt (seeded 2 and 4), have more to do with currying favor with French television than with actual standings were rejected by organizers. "Absolute nonsense," an official retorted. "We looked at world rankings, past records and form on this surface."

This does not explain top-seed American Amelia Earhart, whose best results have not been on any surface at all. Nor does it explain why world number 2 Virginia Stephen-Woolf is seeded 7, world number 1 Anna Pavlova is seeded 3, world number 5 Greta Garbo (Gustafsson) is seeded 8 and world number 6 Tallulah Bankhead is unseeded although, as she says, the tournament doesn't start until Monday.

The US camp was rocked tonight when top junior Bill Burroughs, here with boy wonder Jerry Salinger to provide practice for the Americans, returned a positive swab following routine drug tests. His coach, Ernie Hemingway, was furious with his charge when reporters caught up with him. "I don't know what went wrong," said Hemingway. "We were like father and son."

"It was never going to work," said Burroughs. "We were like father and son."

Burroughs tested positive to every one of twelve banned substances and left this evening in disgrace but unrepentant. "It's ridiculous," he said. "You're expected to perform above yourself but you're not allowed to get there. The system's fucked."

"The day Burroughs knows anything about systems there'll be a blue moon in the sky," said Hemingway, "rather than a sun. The sun is always there. It was there yesterday. And again today."

"Hemingway is fucked," growled Burroughs. "A guy who spends his spare time blowing away elks is not a well-balanced guy. Face it, the man's a fruitcake."

"Burroughs is a self-destructive little faggot," said Hemingway, "and everybody knows it."

"This is great stuff, Ernie," said Burroughs. "I'd get it down while you're still sober and alive."

An hour later American Davis Cup captain Butch Whitman released a statement aimed at steadying the US camp. He made it clear that he was the captain, that Burroughs' behavior had been unacceptable and that there could be no tolerance in such matters. Hemingway was also out of order, he said, in publicly disparaging the sexual orientation of another player. "This was not at issue and neither should it be. This is your captain speaking."

Whitman also had a problem with the other young sparring partner, Jerry Salinger, who burst upon the scene when he took out the American Schools Championship and then a fortnight later won the Junior US Open, the only tournament he has played since. Suggestions that he has been here for a week, practicing at a private resort in the hills, were quickly dispelled by a statement from his home in Connecticut, saying that he had "no interest whatever" in playing, and would not even watch the event on television. When organizers asked to speak to him, however, they were told he had gone out for a Coke.

"If he is here," said Whitman, "I am his captain."

The weather was beautiful here today as the qualifying matches were completed and the champagne opening was declared a huge success.

The full draw in both the men's and women's singles was posted early this evening. Unfortunately world number 6 American Gary Cooper has withdrawn from the tournament because "there's something I've got to do." Otherwise the big news was the drawing of powerful Austrian Gustav Mahler to play Tony Chekhov in a first-round match which will no doubt attract a huge audience.

Organizers are also expected to announce a first-round bye following the mercurial Belgian René Magritte's claim that he had already conducted his opening match on a train.

"This is not possible," said tournament referee Charles Darwin.

"It is possible," Magritte replied. "I have a picture of it."

"This is not within the rules of a tennis tournament."

"This is not a tennis tournament," he replied.

"And get that bag off your head," said Darwin. "You're not funny."

"I beg to differ," said the unassuming Belgian.

Round
1

Day 2

Bernhardt v. Blyton • Baker v. Lillie • Toulouse-Lautrec v. József • Duchamp v. Milne • Sartre v. Ellington • Einstein v. Arp • Hitchcock v. Waller • Maugham v. Fields • Thorndike v. Klein • Astor v. Millay • Luxemburg v. Riefenstahl • Wodehouse v. Scriabin • Fermi v. Toscanini • Joyce v. Bartók

Friedrich Nietzsche, president and CEO of Nike, put it well when he was interviewed on television. "There is a real sense of occasion about this tournament; the best of the older players are still good enough to mix it with the fast rising younger ones. It's a chance to see the absolute cream."

"What about the outlook for the game?"

"Never been better. It's huge," he said. "We're going into Poland, the Low Countries, North Africa, Valhalla, you name it."

"Russia?"

"Ah! Now you mustn't get me on that one. See our legal people about that sort of thing."

"Thank you very much."

"See Gayle."

"Pardon?"

"Have a word with Gayle, she knows all about these things."

There were mixed fortunes for the French on an exciting opening day in ideal conditions. Sarah Bernhardt was business-like against English hope Enid Blyton, and two US-born Parisians Jo Baker and Sylvia Beach had good wins, the exotic Baker seeing off brilliant Canadian Beatrice Lillie who played the match in skates and very nearly won it. Bernhardt described her match as "a good hit-out although the real battle here will be against the Germans."

Baker agrees but is also wary of the Americans. "If you're black and a woman," she says, "you can't be too careful of the Americans."

In the early match on Centre Court, pocket battleship Henri Toulouse-Lautrec accounted for little-known Hungarian Attila József, who played in bare feet and may have thrown himself by taking issue with the custom of taking new balls after five games. "There is no need for new balls," he said. "It is completely unnecessary. These balls are perfectly all right. There are people starving half a kilometer from the stadium and we're using new balls because they look fluffier? Don't give me the shits, please."

And there was a regulation workout on Court 15 for Marcel

Duchamp, the rostered sparring partner on this occasion being the tidy Englishman Alan Milne. Milne has a wonderful capacity for rhythm but Duchamp spotted this and jumped him. Bending his knees to hit the ball late in the first set, standing up and taking it early in the second, Duchamp bewildered his opponent at every turn, waiting for him to mount an attack and then systematically dismantling it. Milne understood exactly what had happened:

> "I have rhythm when I play tennis.
> We finished the first set, Duchamp and I.
> Why am I losing, Duchamp? I asked him.
> You need variation, Duchamp replied.
> But nursie wouldn't like that, I said to Duchamp.
> Nursie wouldn't know, he said. Tell a little lie.
> I lost the second set when we were out playing
> And then I lost the third and saw the rhythm in the score.
> Nursie would be pleased. Nursie would be saying,
> Alan lost to Duchamp, 6–4, 6–4, 6–4."

Duchamp had a heavily strapped thigh and was delighted to win in three. He has been practicing with versatile doubles partner Sam Beckett, the Irish cricketer, cyclist and chess player. Seeded 2 in the doubles, they claim to be incapable of winning but impossible to defeat. Their practice session today consisted of a brief discussion, some drawings on a napkin and a good-natured dispute about whose turn it was to get the cigarettes.

In less sparkling form was French Davis Cup specialist Jean-Paul Sartre, lucky to scramble to a win over talented American Duke Ellington on Court 2. Ellington made a lot of friends today, Sartre very few indeed. He refuses to compete outside France and even in his own national championship has been known to issue alternative statements of results. He contested line calls, corrected the umpire's interpretation of the rules and on several occasions smashed the ball straight at his opponent.

Ellington doesn't predict great things for Sartre. "I don't think he can see properly," he said. "Look at the way he played. I nearly beat him and I took up the game only six months ago. I'm really in Paris because I want to check out a sideman, and if you'll excuse me I'm already late."

Earlier in the day warm favorite Albert Einstein never got out of a trot in dispatching the abstracted Frenchman Jean Arp. Described by friends as a thinker, the affable German with exploding hair had a meteoric career as a junior, highlighted by a win in the Swiss Open two weeks short of his seventeenth birthday.

"His ground strokes are miraculous," commented sometime doubles partner, Italian Enrico Fermi. "And he seems to have all the time in the world to play them."

Einstein has a ballistic first service, unofficially clocked at 400 kilometers per hour, which he refuses to use in competition. "Someone could get hurt," he said. There is a joke on the tour that one of these days he'll be seeded twice in the same tournament, which he concedes is a little unusual "but not impossible, provided the seedings are moving with a uniform velocity."

Even though he double-faulted sixteen times today and triple-faulted once in controversial circumstances, he never looked like being broken, while Arp's service was under constant pressure. In the third set Einstein persistently ran around his forehand and flicked the ball back over Arp's head as he rushed the net. "There's a blind spot just behind the left shoulder as you're moving in. If you can land the ball there, your opponent can't see it at all."

"That's right," confirmed Arp later. "I'd serve and come in and the ball would disappear. I couldn't tell where the hell it had gone."

"It hadn't gone anywhere," said Einstein. "You just couldn't see it."

"I could hear it," said Arp.

"Ah, then it hadn't gone," said Einstein.

"I didn't say it had gone," said Arp. "I said I couldn't tell where it had gone."

"That's my point," said Einstein.

"I think you'll find that's *my* point, Albert," said Arp.

"Fifteen-all," said Einstein and began to giggle.

On the outside courts, the slightly eerie Fred Hitchcock was bundled out in straight sets by a handy black American luxuriating in the unlikely name of Fats Waller, who played like a young man in a big hurry.

But perhaps the biggest news was Willie Maugham, beaten by American Bill Fields in a seesawing match notable more for the number of shots than for their quality. Maugham afterwards complained that Fields' hat would sometimes rise several centimeters in the air as he was preparing to serve.

"What's the man talking about?" said Fields. "When I'm preparing to serve, everything is moving: Willie, the ball, the net, the crowd, the court and the suburb. The wonder is that I can serve at all. Did I ever tell you about the time I fell out of an aircraft during a lapse in concentration? Whose deal is it?"

In the women's draw a somewhat imperious Sybil Thorndike was tied up in knots by Austrian tactician Melanie Klein, and the profligate Nancy Astor was toppled by Edna St. Vincent Millay, who was in great touch despite her habit of burning the candle at both ends. "I had sex before the match," she confided, "so I'm pretty tired. Fortunately it didn't affect my performance and most of the men played well today too."

Polish dark-horse Rosa Luxemburg created the sensation of the day by ousting lanky German number 1 Leni Riefenstahl. Her entire national hierarchy turned out to see Riefenstahl, who was in terrific form. She looked great, her court coverage was excellent and she accepted flowers from the German administration after winning the first set 6–2. Luxemburg waited for her to put the flowers down and then took her apart. She was virtually camped at the net for the second set and by the third she was in control.

As the relationship between the sun and the yardarm was reflected in a more relaxed atmosphere, the New York Englishman Plum Wodehouse, equipped with long trousers and sneakers, prevailed over the big-serving Russian Aleksandr Scriabin, by simply getting the ball back. "Isn't that the general idea?" asked Wodehouse. "I'm afraid you'll have to excuse me if I've missed the point."

"What was I supposed to do?" said Scriabin. "I hit the ball at a hundred kilometers an hour and it drifted back at twenty-five. Doesn't do that in practice."

"It's very nearly a nine iron from behind the baseline," said Wodehouse, "with just the slightest suggestion of fade."

And there was plenty of other action. Fermi was slow to start against his talented countryman Arturo Toscanini but once he got his serve working all Toscanini could do was point her up into the wind and radio for help.

Fermi requested a ruling about whether "on" the line was "in," in the same sense that "on the line" was "in the line."

"If you have a ball, for instance," he said, "which is clearly out, and which marks the ground outside the line, but which brings up dust, having struck the outer extremity of the line with its inner extremity, can it not be said that dust is the criterion, rather than the inness or the outness? I think we should be clear about these things."

In the highlight of the evening session James Joyce, the Irishman who spends so much time in France he's practically a local, won an epic struggle against Hungarian Davis Cup captain Béla Bartók. Joyce lost concentration when he was cautioned in the third set for foul language. After a crosscourt winner was called out during a tie-break he swore solidly for twenty minutes without once repeating himself. His imagery was drawn from a great many sources and in particular the religious beliefs of the Gibraltan umpire were subjected to fierce ridicule. Many patrons walked out as the language became more offensive, although those who left were quickly replaced by others who made notes and met afterwards to develop a closer reading.

Sitting in the players' box, unpredictable Czech doubles specialist Tristan Tzara said afterwards he'd never heard anything like it. "I shared a house with Jimmy at one stage and he's a great guy, but you've really got to get out of the way when he gets dirty. I've heard him talking to his wife too and that is completely disgusting."

Bartók said he had played Joyce before. Joyce agreed but made the useful point that he had never played Bartók.

Day 3

Proust v. Synge • Bakst v. Bierce • Brecht v. Koestler • de Beauvoir v. Garden • Nijinsky v. Lubitsch • Chaliapin v. Jung • Carmichael v. Lorca

The French got away to a much healthier start this morning with a gritty win to Marcel Proust over the Irishman John Synge. The crowd went nuts and there is no doubt the French show is now on the road. This was a danger match for Proust and is an excellent result. How much it took out of him remains to be seen. He's in a tough section of the draw and he won't want too many affairs that go to 11–9 in the fifth.

Russian pinup boy Leon Bakst was tipped out of the competition by the experienced American eccentric Ambrose Bierce, who took to him right from the start. "I thought I'd better get on with it," he said. "He hits the ball well but there are plenty of dead marksmen on a battlefield."

Furious at the result, Bakst refused to attend the press conference and it was left to Bierce to explain what might have gone wrong. "I naturally assume if a man is said to have the best forehand in the game, he must have a weak forehand. He's used to people tiptoeing around his forehand as if it's possessed of magical powers. The hell it is. Let's slam a few in there."

In the first set Bierce served exclusively to the Bakst forehand and played all his lobs and drop shots into the forehand court. The Russian watched his forehand fall apart.

"It didn't fall apart," said Bierce. "He didn't have one."

"He has one against anyone else," opined Norman Mailer.

"And was he playing anyone else, hugebrain?" said Bierce, who goes through to meet the colorful customs officer Rousseau in a second-round matchup commentators are already describing as "Beauty and the Beast."

Much-touted Berliner Bertolt Brecht went out to Hungarian Arthur Koestler. Near the end of the fourth set Brecht tore his shirt off and screamed, "I am not a tennis player or an entertainer. I am a man," which, as Koestler later said, "wasn't as surprising as he obviously thought it was."

Brecht didn't seem too bothered by the loss. "I have no interest whatever in the rankings and I care nothing for money. It is a means of oppression and I've got plenty of it in America anyway."

In the early afternoon Scotland's voluble Mary Garden ma an early exit against Simone de Beauvoir. An American frien of de Beauvoir, Mr. Nelson Algren, was cautioned for comment he made from the players' box.

"You bitch," he said after she won the first set. "You heartless cow," he added after she broke Garden in the second.

"Listen! Fuck you, Nelson!" responded de Beauvoir.

She was penalized a point.

"No!" she protested. "Why should I have to put up with this shit?"

"Because I have to," said Mr. Algren, who then rose and removed himself from the box.

Facilities out at Court 13 simply couldn't cope during Polish whiz-kid Vaslav Nijinsky's match with the methodical German Ernst Lubitsch. Nijinsky is a joy to watch. He has the full sack of tools, astonishing leg strength and court coverage bordering on the supernatural. He is listed to play doubles with the Russian Serge Diaghilev although rumors of a split have been in currency all week and they have not trained together since Tuesday, Nijinsky instead spending time with his young wife and Diaghilev with the sort of Russians who speak French and the sort of French who put Dreyfus away.

In another highlight of the afternoon Fyodor Chaliapin, who is as strong around the baseline as anyone in the game today, took a set from animated Swiss number 1 Carl Jung, but could do little to delay the inevitable and lost in four.

"I remember seeing a game of tennis as a child," said Jung. "I think it was on a beach. There were rocks and sand but otherwise it was very like this. It seems to be a kind of ritual. There are equivalents in other cultures, of course, although I doubt that any of them would avail us of the excellent prospect of spending a couple of hours under a westering sun with a fellow like Fyodor."

And there was lively work on Court 16 where Hoagy Carmichael played intelligent tennis to hold out Fred Lorca, the gifted Spaniard who has had such trouble establishing himself in his own country. Carmichael plays down his all-round ability by saying he's "not good at anything in particular." He describes his serve as "ramshackle" and his ground strokes as "an honest attempt." Asked how he felt after the match, he said, "How do you think I feel? I used to be a lawyer in Indiana and here I am in Paris doing this. I feel marvelous."

After two days of first-round matches, betting markets are wide open. The women's looks like a Bernhardt–de Beauvoir benefit but support has come in for Sarojini Naidu, Lillian Hellman and Willa Cather after good early showings. Ladbrokes say Einstein has firmed but there is plenty of money about for Sartre and late this afternoon a plunge on Beiderbecke brought him in from 40s to 12s.

Van Gogh will have his odds slashed if he dispatches Constantine Cavafy. At 20s he was worth a nibble but the sports journalists have given it just short of a thrashing ever since. Wally

Benjamin was shunted in from 200s to 12s, although these odds may flatter him. Anybody looking for an investment should consider Picasso at 30s, Maurice Ravel at 100s and the quiet American Cummings at 300–1. There is support for SuperTom Eliot but at 8–4 he is unbackable and will drift.

The shorteners tomorrow will be Vladimir Nabokov, if he can get past the obstreperous Henry Miller, and the insouciant Waller, who rear-windowed Hitchcock this morning.

Day 4

Melba v. Luce • Colette v. Kahlo • de Chirico v. Moore • Yeats v. Klimt • Chekhov v. Mahler • Tolstoy v. Kokoschka • Gropius v. Hasek • Léger v. Runyon • Gödel v. Spender • Mandelstam v. Reed • Hemingway v. Visconti

"How do I think it's going?" asked Wilde. "I've never seen anything like it on a first day. And only very seldom on a first night." Mr. Wilde is here as an observer. "It was either that or come here simply to watch," he says.

He and his friend Mr. Whistler do not play tennis. "One should never perspire in white," opines Whistler, although Wilde once boxed for Ireland ("as indeed who hasn't").

The pair gave a press conference which began at 5:30, broke for dinner at eight, recommenced at ten and is already regarded as having the best first act in the history of modern media.

"Are you with the official party?" Wilde was asked.

"No," replied Wilde, "I'm with Whistler."

Was Mr. Whistler with the official party?

"No," replied Whistler. "But I have a cousin in shipping."

"This really is a marvelous occasion," said Wilde. "I'm beginning to wish I'd entered."

"You will, Oscar," said Whistler. "You will."

There was action aplenty this morning. Rosa Luxemburg, the American Anna Strong and Latvia's Lina Stern announced that they did not wish to play for their countries. "It's a complete distortion," said Luxemburg. "And a trap."

"Has anyone noticed we're run by the *World* Tennis Organization?" demanded Strong sternly. "This is an *international* body. And they make us compete for our separate nations?"

"Who cares which country wins?" agreed Stern strongly. "We're being exploited."

"What we need," said Luxemburg, "is proper government of the game by a central authority elected by all the players, not a coven of pimps controlled by international corporations and media."

"What are any of us doing in this ridiculous competition?" asked Strong. "I should be doing my work, back in China, coaching."

"Then why are you here?" demanded Emmeline Pankhurst.

"You, of all people, should know that, Emmeline," said

Luxemburg. "Do you think we'd be having this press conference if we hadn't come to Paris?"

"Why did you chain yourself to the British parliament?" inquired Stern. "Wasn't it one of your people who disrupted the Derby?"

"True," conceded Pankhurst. "But I'm supporting England in this tournament."

"You're obviously looking for a job in management," said Strong, "by pretending to be a threat to the system."

"How dare you!" said Pankhurst. "I'll have you know I—"

"Fuck off, Emily," said Luxemburg. "Go back to your knitting."

This exchange rather overshadowed irresistible performances from Americans Mae West, Ruth Draper and Dorothy Parker, to say nothing of a jaw-dropper by the Australian Nellie Melba, who was down a break in both sets against Clare Boothe Luce but came back each time.

Playing with a brace on her back following a car accident and bandaging to both knees "after a weekend away with Trotsky," fancied Mexican Frida Kahlo was always going to lack court speed in her match with Colette Claudine.

Colette disguised her shots nicely and Kahlo was relieved when it was over. "It was killing me," she said. "I was only doing it for Diego. I am in pain but the coffee mugs are selling well."

It was business as usual for the men, with one exception. The scoreboard at Court 4 this morning read "G. de Chirico (Hel) v. G. Moore (Ire)." The umpire sat in his chair and the linespeople stood at their posts as the players came out. A voice somewhere yelled, "Go Giorgio!" and another answered, "We want Moore!" Laughter rippled around the court as people applied sunscreen and made themselves comfortable.

They needn't have bothered. The great perfectionist, Giorgio de Chirico, turned up in spotless whites and lodged a formal complaint. Moore's clothing bore the manufacturer's labels on the outside, he said. This bespoke a moral weakness. "I have no interest in appearing on the same court as a degenerate. I shall be in my room. Let me know when you've got this business sorted out."

"What century is this?" asked Moore. "Everybody wears clothing with sponsors' names on it."

"If a million people do a stupid thing, it is still a stupid thing," said de Chirico. "Good sense is not democratic any more than good health is. You want to wake up to yourself, Moore."

"If you think my shirt is distracting," said Moore, "you're going to need oxygen when you see my tennis."

"I have no intention of seeing your tennis, as you call it," said de Chirico. "I am concerned only with seeing the ball."

"I'll endeavor to play slowly," said Moore.

Meanwhile, Moore's friend Big Bill Yeats was in trouble early against the Austrian Gustav Klimt before finding some rhythm but he doesn't look the player of previous years, and it was only when his longtime friend Maud Gonne was absent during the tie-break in the second set that he began to concentrate. He tore off four unplayable serves and returned Klimt's with ease, winning the tie-break to love. Gonne returned shortly afterwards but then Ludwig Wittgenstein's sister turned up and Klimt lost control of his serve.

The storm worsened for Austria across what became a productive morning for Russian tennis. The indefatigable Chekhov looked commanding against Mahler and the Count, Leo Tolstoy, had far too much for Oscar Kokoschka.

Mahler pumped himself up between points and made great drama out of line calls and bad shots, carrying on as if he'd been harpooned when he left a Chekhovian crosscourt return, only to see it drop in. The Mahler serve is so strong its power dominates even Mahler himself. After winning the second set he waved to the big German section of the crowd and stood with his hands in the air, his face set in defiance, his shadow thrown deep across the court. When this display was over, Chekhov carried on as if absolutely nothing had happened. Mahler's wife, Alma, was in the players' box at the beginning of the match but had vacated it by the end. Chekhov suggested she might have gone to Moscow but Mahler wasn't convinced.

It wasn't an easy morning for players' wives. When Anna Tolstoy arrived for husband Leo's match the players' box was full of other women, at least two of whom were on her own staff. Tolstoy suggested these women may have been there to support Kokoschka. This didn't look likely since the young women were clearly rooting for the Count.

Alma Mahler also had her hands full, monitoring the progress of her companion Kokoschka, checking on Court 17, where Walter Gropius was in all sorts of trouble against Hasek, dashing to Court 4 where Austria's Franz Werfel was working on his service action, and visiting the recovery room where Gustav was complaining of a corked thigh. Kokoschka was upset by a line call at 2–0 in the second set and by the time Alma returned he was accusing the umpire of footfaulting him because he wasn't a freemason. It was all downhill from there.

The locals turned out this afternoon to cheer Fernand Léger, one of the few players to have a two-handed backhand, a two-handed forehand and a two-handed service. He sometimes drives the ball wide but well and seems torn between the mathematical disadvantage occasioned by the loss of a point and the mechanical efficiency of striking the ball truly.

The American Damon Runyon comes largely unheralded, although if we can judge by the number of scribes with plenty of 40–1 on him to reach the quarterfinals, there is some chance he knows what he is doing. Léger romped out to 6–2, 6–2 and, at the changeover at 5–0 in the third, Runyon told the umpire to get on him quickly since the odds were excellent and he had worked his opponent out. His good humor endeared him to the parochial crowd and nobody minded when he took the third and found another gear in the fourth to take it 6–1. At 5–0 in the fifth he offered to take any amount of anyone's money on Léger at 50–1. This motion lapsed for want of a seconder and he served out the business at 6–0.

There was better news for Austria on Court 11 where the

very calculating Kurt Gödel looked in wonderful form against the attractive young Englishman Stephen Spender, although he seemed distracted by the umpire's call at 1–1 in the third set.

"What's the problem?" asked the umpire.

"How many games have we played in this set?" asked Gödel.

"Two," said the umpire.

"And we've won one each?" said Gödel.

"That's right. Is there some difficulty with that?"

"I take it you imagine one and one to be two."

"If you're going to question that," said the umpire, "you'll be flying in the face of every mathematician since Euclid."

"Euclid believed the world was flat," replied Gödel. "Euclidean ideas cannot be axiomatic."

"Until someone can prove that one and one are not two, I'll operate on the assumption that they are."

"It is not necessary to prove that one and one are not two. It is necessary only that there be an instance in which it cannot be proven that they *are*."

"We've played two games in this set," repeated the umpire, "and the score is one all."

"This is all very fine as an assertion," said Gödel. "What I am concerned about is verifiable proof."

Also through to the second round today were the majestic Russian Osip Mandelstam and the Norwegian Eddie Munch, who looks as if he couldn't pull the skin off a rice pudding. Mandelstam is a joy to watch and today he made just two unforced errors against the polished Englishman Carol Reed, only the third man this year to take a set from the Russian.

The Rules Committee announced this evening that, in order to clarify the situation, the following pairings have been removed from the mixed doubles:

F. Werfel (Aut) and A. Mahler (Aut)

W. Gropius (Ger) and A. Mahler (Aut)

G. Mahler (Aut) and A. Mahler (Aut)

O. Kokoschka (Aut) and A. Mahler (Aut).

There was one other withdrawal from the mixed: the W. B. Yeats (Ire) and M. Gonne-MacBride (Ire) combination will not be competing because, as Yeats put it, "No point. She won't play."

Meanwhile Ernie Hemingway had a good hit-out tonight against panoramic Italian Luchino Visconti. Gertrude Stein watched from the players' box until Hemingway was forced to deny that she was coaching him by the use of hand signals.

"I was tired," he said. "I didn't need the old woman telling me what to do. She wanted to help. I could see that. Could see it in her eyes. Something in me said, 'Yes.' Something else said, 'No.' I went with the 'no.' I forget where the sun was. 'Up' probably."

Day 5

Earhart v. O'Keeffe • Christie v. Oakley • Akhmatova v. Buck • Chanel v. Bara • Pickford v. Post • Gide v. Freud • Crosby v. Coward • Stanislavsky v. Picasso • Forster v. Pirandello • Miller v. Matisse • Wittgenstein v. Williams

Five women's seeds were on court today and all went through. Amelia Earhart was a picture of efficiency in her win over countrywoman Georgia O'Keeffe. This was a contrast in styles, Earhart in shorts and playing a strong serve and volley game, O'Keeffe in flowing drapery which fell, at rest, like soft flower petals arranged in the form of a vagina.

Agatha Christie posed questions to which the normally accurate Annie Oakley simply didn't have the answers. The Russian Anna Akhmatova had a good battle against Pearl Buck and, whatever was needed against the American Theda Bara, Coco Chanel had it. On Court 3, in an all-American derby, Mary Pickford shat on Emily Post.

The crowd was put through the agonies of St. Jude by the brilliant but often frustrating Frenchman André Gide. The Austrian Sigmund Freud, who may have to be spoken to about his loud grunts, said Gide must have seen his parents in the act of congress. Gide replied that his parents were dead but the Doc insisted: "Gide must have imagined his parents in the act of congress. It was not important how he saw them in the act of congress, simply that he did."

Gide was unmoved. It had never occurred to him, he said, that his parents engaged in congress at all. He described himself as a married gay red anti-communist Christian revolutionary hedonist ascetic and countered that, since it was Freud's idea that his parents had experienced congress, it must have been Freud who imagined it.

Next up, we saw Bing Crosby happily trouncing Noel Coward. A natural with something of Twain about him (he whistles to himself while changing ends), Crosby was untroubled by the technically accomplished Coward, who made no excuses but is well known to prefer playing doubles "in which we serve slightly better."

Constantin Stanislavsky's method of playing is "to analyze the psychology" of the player he wishes to be and, by sheer concentration, then "become" that player. "I am not being me," he says. "I must actually become someone else." Precisely who he was being in his contest against Picasso was not obvious but after the second set he made a number of guttural remarks and banged himself on the head with an ice bucket. This seemed to clarify things and he took the third set before Picasso got down to business.

Until recently Picasso autographed his racquets after a match and threw them into the crowd. Those lucky enough to catch one were making up to $500 each from fans anxious to purchase a memento of their hero. WTO officials lowered the boom when it became clear that the same people were catching the racquets at each tournament and upon closer inspection proved to be employed as racquet-catchers by Picasso's company, Racquets Inc. The Spaniard loves the Centre Court atmosphere and was still out there signing autographs when the players were hitting up for the next match.

The English Davis Cup selectors took a keen interest in Ted Forster's tussle with accomplished Italian Luigi Pirandello but, the minute Forster noticed them conferring, the pressure seemed to get to him. "I heard what the women were saying yesterday," he confessed. "I don't want to be in some national squad either. This is not a team sport. It's an individual thing."

The fact remains that very few other English players could take a game by the scruff of the neck the way Forster did this afternoon for the first set and a half. Pirandello fought back in the second, which he won 6–4 before asking if the line judges wanted to play, since, he said, there seemed no reason why they shouldn't.

"Quiet please, Mr. Pirandello," said the umpire. "The crowd has come here to see you."

"The crowd has come here to see whatever occurs," said Pirandello.

"They have come to see you two play," said the umpire.

"Do we need a ball?" asked Pirandello.

"Of course you need a ball," said the umpire. "Tennis is a ball game."

"Ah! But could they not imagine a ball?"

"Don't be silly," said Forster, "everybody might imagine a different ball. That, surely, is the reason we are using a real ball."

"You're a big help, Ted," said Pirandello. "I don't go around poking holes in your half-baked ideas. I'll thank you to stay out of it."

"I'm sorry," said Forster. "I think you'll find the rules are clear on this point."

"You're about as radical as a chocolate frog. The first time the rules look threatened, you're in there defending them."

"Rubbish," replied Forster.

"Why don't you just tell the officials you're gay?" asked Pirandello.

"I do. In private."

What a pity that young Arthur Miller and perennial favorite Henri Matisse had to come up against one another. The American took the first set easily, setting his points up well, maneuvering Matisse out of position and making it look elementary. As somebody said, it was the best mix of brains and power we've seen so far. Matisse lifted in the second, however, scrambling for everything to stay in the match. Miller won the third in a tie-break but Matisse came back again and the fourth set was the pick of the litter. Miller threw everything at it and Matisse, who came to the net only three times all day, slowly took control from the baseline, hitting a purple patch at 0–4 down and getting it to 6–6. When he won the set in a tie-break the crowd erupted.

In the final set there was only one service break, Matisse hitting four consecutive winners from Miller's rocketry to go to 4–2 and that was the match. It is a good thing that Miller is playing doubles. He is a very impressive young man.

Ludwig Wittgenstein taught himself to play while in the army and has come from nowhere to take his country's number 1 Davis Cup singles berth from Kurt Gödel. A handful for many on the tour because of his unusual behavior, Wittgenstein apologizes when he wins a match and questions line calls when he feels he has been given an unfair advantage. Some players have accused him of doing this to disrupt the rhythm of the match.

"This is quite true," says Wittgenstein. "I do it in order to break my concentration. I'm sorry if others are affected. Perhaps I will retire. You're not writing this down, are you?"

William Carlos Williams did little wrong against him in the first set, produced pure poetry in the second and looked invincible at 5–0 in the third. What Wittgenstein had been doing up until this point was not clear but he broke Williams to love and took the next six games and the final three sets with an astonishing array of shots against which it was impossible to mount any kind of defense.

Wittgenstein said he was "not pleased" with the way he played today and lodged a formal protest over the result. "Williams won more games than I did. It seems grossly unfair that he should lose."

Day 6

Miller v. Lardner • Berryman v. Hecht • Grosz v. Prokofiev • Strindberg v. Hardy • Stein v. Hari • Stephen-Woolf v. Schiaparelli • Canetti v. Beckett

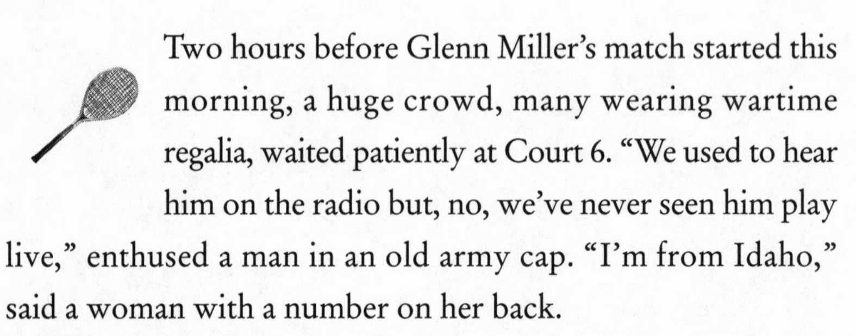

Two hours before Glenn Miller's match started this morning, a huge crowd, many wearing wartime regalia, waited patiently at Court 6. "We used to hear him on the radio but, no, we've never seen him play live," enthused a man in an old army cap. "I'm from Idaho," said a woman with a number on her back.

When Miller came out with his opponent Ring Lardner the place went mad. Hats were tossed in the air, whistles were blown and several couples had to be restrained from dancing on the court. It must be said the crowd's interest in the tennis was less than forensic. It didn't matter what their man did, they cheered. He won the first set and they went wild. In the second he lost his way and they went just as wild. Lardner, playing beautifully now, took the next two and the match, and the crowd went wild again.

The thing about Miller is that he can be moving in completely the wrong direction and his people don't care, their heads are bobbing with the rhythm. He can play the same shot six or seven times in a row; they don't care. He can, as he did at one point, just stand there shuffling his feet for a while, and they all stand up and shuffle their feet. No crowd ever left a court happier and their man had just been defeated.

Lardner is a class act and might ruffle a few feathers here. Miller had no excuses. "I was going along all right. I just went missing. I don't know what went wrong."

John Berryman turned up this morning wearing someone else's clothing and clutching a racquet lent to him by the child of a concierge. His opponent Ben Hecht walked him around a bit and gave him plenty of water before the match started, and then Berryman reeled off ten straight games. He was sharp, he moved well, he had it on a string. Hecht had to resign himself to wait. The steam went out of the Berryman serve at about 2-all in the third and he began to lose interest. The longer the match went, the more interest he lost. By the end, he had lost all interest.

There was also tragedy on Court 6 this morning for German-American George Grosz, who was stretchered off following a very nasty fall. He was leaping for an overhead when he seemed to lose balance and plunged to the ground. He had been playing well and was on terms in his match with Russian Sergei Prokofiev.

"It is always the way," said Prokofiev. "I got through to the fourth round in the Russian championship one year and by the time I got home my cat was dead, my bicycle had been stolen and I was being denounced as a decadent formalist."

In a shock result on an outside court, August Strindberg, another of the brilliant Swedes, was filleted by the wily Englishman Thomas Hardy. Play was delayed when a waitress was fired for dropping a tray of drinks in one of the hospitality areas. Hardy approached the umpire and asked if there wasn't something they could do to help the young woman.

As the incident had occurred outside the court and between points, the umpire explained, it was outside his jurisdiction.

Hardy submitted that, since play had been delayed to accommodate the incident, and since the incident was witnessed by the entire crowd, it was, in terms of time and structure, part of the match; therefore the rules of the game should apply. The young woman should be recalled and the drinks served again.

The umpire summoned Strindberg and explained that the match referee could be consulted if it were the wish of both players.

"What's the point?" said Strindberg.

"The man is asking whether we should get the match referee," said Hardy. "The obvious answer is 'yes.'"

"There is no answer," said Strindberg. "Life is hideous."

"Play," said the umpire.

But Hardy's mind was elsewhere. He served eight consecutive double faults and made little effort to return Strindberg's service. Strindberg took the set 6–1 and Hardy sat for a long time with a towel over his head before coming out again. He played like a different man. Midway through the third set the despondent Swede was banging his racquet on the ground and conversing with the sky on a range of issues.

Two seeded women went through today. Gertrude Stein was in trouble early against exotic Dutchwoman Mata Hari, who spun a web over the first set, and it took every bit of the American's strength to get out from under it. "A win is a win is a win," said Stein. "I played well enough just well enough yes well enough and well enough."

Virginia Stephen-Woolf had an easier time with the stylish Italian Elsa Schiaparelli and spoke after the match of having seen Sarah Bernhardt practicing. "She is magnificent and what a booming serve. It's so very hard to get good service these days."

But was she happy with the way she played?

"Not bad. But it would be nice to get a boom of one's own."

There were plenty of empty seats out on Court 1 tonight for the match between Elias Canetti and Sam Beckett. A solitary bare tree stood against the sky and the contest began bleakly for Beckett, the Bulgarian passing him on both sides at will.

"If he works out what you're thinking," Beckett said later, "he can take you apart." But Beckett was nothing if not patient. He waited. In fact waiting probably won him the match because by the time he'd finished waiting he was hitting the ball beautifully.

"I was lucky," said Beckett.

"I couldn't work out what he was thinking," said Canetti.

"I wasn't thinking anything," said Beckett.

"Nothing?" asked Canetti.

"No. Not nothing," said Beckett. "I wasn't thinking anything at all."

Day 7

Mead v. Duncan • Disney v. Strachey • Cavafy v. van Gogh • Chandler v. Rodo

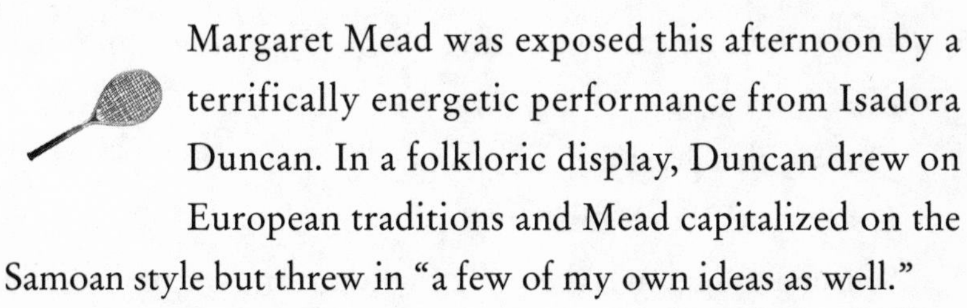

Margaret Mead was exposed this afternoon by a terrifically energetic performance from Isadora Duncan. In a folkloric display, Duncan drew on European traditions and Mead capitalized on the Samoan style but threw in "a few of my own ideas as well."

Duncan was delighted with her win although if she keeps playing in long flowing robes she runs the risk of serious injury. "It feels fantastic," she said. "I feel like a river running." She may feel like a river but she has only to step on her own hem while accelerating across court and the flow will slow to a trickle. Great to watch but fraught with danger.

The feature match of the morning session was unfortunately something of a fizzer. American college sensation Walt Disney has won more money on the tour in the past year than his opponent today has made in his life. He has sponsorship deals running out his ears and knows only one type of game, which he describes as "winning." He may have to put his game on ice for a while after the sobering experience of "winning" only two games against Lytton Strachey, a gangling Englishman to whom he hardly spoke.

Celebrity guest Oscar Wilde reported that he and his friend Whistler are "enjoying proceedings enormously. We love the tennis and we've just had some blueberries. As I've always suspected, Whistler is a confirmed Blueberryist."

"The blueberries you eat?"

"One doesn't eat blueberries. One drifts through schools of them, mouth open. Blueberries are the plankton of the high teas."

"How can one eat something without putting it in one's mouth?"

"Only with a great deal of practice."

"It seems self-contradictory."

"Self-contradiction is the soul of wisdom and the basis of the British postal system."

"The British postal system? How so?"

"Every day millions of envelopes are placed in mailboxes. Indeed I'm told this occurs even in parts of Shropshire. Each envelope displays an address which, by virtue of being elsewhere, is the direct opposite of the location of the mailbox. It is this contradiction to which the postal system must . . ."

"Address itself?" speculated Whistler.

"Exactly so."

In the highlight of the day's live television coverage, we saw the Egyptian-born Greek Cavafy from Alexandria up against Holland's Vincent van Gogh, who lives in Arles and is regarded by many as French. Vangers is regarded by many as the best player never to win a grand slam tournament. Plagued by ear problems which have affected his balance and by balance troubles which have affected his ear, he has career prize money to date of nil. He began wildly, returning service by rocking back onto his right foot and belting the ball with astonishing power as high in the air as he could. If it came down on his own side of the net, he shouted at it and hit it again. After doing this six times in a row he was spoken to by the umpire.

"Mr. van Gogh," he said. "You must stop it. We are here to play tennis."

"I am playing tennis," said van Gogh.

"You are not playing tennis the way tennis is played," said the umpire.

"I am hitting a tennis ball with a tennis racquet," said the troubled Dutchman, "in tennis clothing, on a tennis court, in a tennis tournament. I am, in fact, currently talking to a tennis umpire."

"You are too wild, too fierce," said the umpire. "Who is your coach?"

"Coach? I play as I see," said van Gogh as he walked back to his place.

Cavafy, for his part, played classical tennis. His racquets were of the small-headed, wooden-framed variety and each was contained within a racquet press. He stood well up to receive but when van Gogh gets onto his serve it can really motor, and time and again the Greek maintained his friezelike position as the ball scorched down the backhand side and slammed into the canvas behind him. After a while, van Gogh's primitive swinging began to produce results and the Cavafy service game, lovely to watch and based on the eternal verities, took on an air of infinite sadness.

There were further shocks for American tennis in the late afternoon. Californian Ray Chandler was on court for two hours and fifty-seven minutes today trying to cut himself free of Uruguayan qualifier José Rodo, who has been critical of the game in America and likes nothing more than an opponent who has done well there. Chandler learned his tennis in England and has good technique coupled with American confidence. Plagued by injuries, he has sometimes missed entire seasons, so is seldom in the business of putting together a demanding fortnight of five-set matches. He lost today, but only just and has lost so many times now he says if he ever won anything he'd walk into a door getting up to collect it.

"Rodo was good," he said. "He had good feet. He got to the ball like an anesthetist with an early tee time. Last night was beginning to look like a bad idea. The 'little sleep' theory needed work and I made a note to talk to the guy in charge of the daylight. Way too bright. I pushed a few back and tried to remember what I was doing here. Everywhere I looked there were people, like extras in some meaningless advertisement. Just faces. And some legs. I preferred the legs.

"I lost a game and got something wet from the courtside fridge. I tried to sip it but I wasn't fooling anyone. The place was a mess. Someone could clean up later. Right now I had to think. I went out again and bent a couple at the guy up the other end. A dame behind me yelled, 'Out.' She was right. It was that sort of a day."

Day 8

Muir v. Galsworthy • Wolfe v. Cummings • Fitzgerald v. Neruda • Nin v. West • Sayers v. Yourcenar • Stopes v. Moore • Porter v. Pankhurst • Pavlova v. Dietrich

It was a treat this morning to watch the resourceful Scot Edwin Muir jump for joy after his unexpected win over big John Galsworthy. "It was like a dream," he said. "A mythological dream of some sort." Muir's main game is to play doubles with his pal Wally Benjamin and if he can pick up a little business in the singles it's always a bonus.

"It's just great to be here," he said in his Robbie Burns brogue. "Fantastic. Och, there are some gae bonny players here the noo. I was watching Bing Crosby wi' Walt Disney on yon practice courts yesterday. Ver' different from ain another but both brilliant."

"What is the difference?" quizzed Mailer, doing the rounds.

"The difference?" said Muir. "Bing sings. But Walt disney."

Americans Tom Wolfe and Ted Cummings, both very fit players of great power, came out and for two and a half hours they stood and delivered. Wolfe has a huge booming serve and Cummings, who serves underarm, has a return as good as any in the game. Their media call after the match was also a contrast in styles. Wolfe spoke for some time about being in Paris for the first time.

Cummings recalled being in France some years ago in baffling circumstances. "I remember an ambulance and a train accident and I think I was arrested and then I was back in every our town blooming in the blossoms in the sweet time is our time is my time six love."

Another rising star to make an appearance today was the popular Scott Fitzgerald, who looks to many Europeans to be the quintessential American and to many Americans like something out of a play. He looked sluggish and there have been suggestions he is suffering from a virus. He was lucky to get home in the first-set tie-break against clay court exponent Pablo Neruda, but after that it was all the Chilean. If you've never seen Chileans celebrate, get along to Neruda's second-round match.

The women's draw offered its own pleasures today. This was no surprise to Anaïs Nin. "The women's draw is pleasure," she said after going down to Rebecca West. "That is its purpose. That is its destiny." West, who came here as a junior (as Cicily Fairfield), was sharp all day and goes through. Nin was full of praise. "She was wonderful," she said of West. "Absolutely wonderful. I'll never forget it."

Dot Sayers, natty in shorts and looking very like a kind of grown-up Christopher Robin, was beaten by Marguerite Yourcenar of Belgium. "How I look is irrelevant," said Sayers. "How I look is how I need to look in order to play the way I play. The way I play is not the way I look. The way I play is the way I think."

The Scot Marie Stopes has one of the best defensive games in the business. American Marianne Moore mounted attack after attack and tried everything in the book but Stopes was impregnable.

An even bigger surprise was Kathy-Anne Porter's demolition of Emmeline Pankhurst. Porter has been knocking on the door for a few years and she arrived in a big way out there today, serving powerfully and never giving the fifth seed a look-in. Pankhurst was as shocked as anyone. "I'm shocked," she said. "I'm probably as shocked as anyone."

The Pavlova–Dietrich affair will be talked about for years. Marlene Dietrich, who left her native Germany as a junior and now plays mainly in the US, is deadly if the crowd gets behind her. This was always going to be interesting because the French crowd adores her but also loves the gifted Russian Anna Pavlova. And the more the crowd loved the match, the better it got. Pavlova's court coverage is astounding and she has electrifying speed. Dietrich is nothing but ground strokes and with Pavlova in full stride all she could do was wait for the music to stop.

"What could I do?" said Dietrich. "I could do nothing. I was so tired."

But Dietrich did do something. She slowed her game down even further. She hit the ball very late and low and she scorched her shots past Pavlova as she came in.

Pavlova was stunned. The fire went out of her game. She became meek and withdrawn. "I felt as if I was dying," she said. "The life was going out of me. It was ebbing away."

Dietrich won the second set and carried all before her again in the third before Pavlova quite suddenly emerged from her chrysalis and began to build to a big finish. She was everywhere. She dashed from side to side like a dervish, she sprinted from the back court to the net and her overheads were breathtaking. In the end Dietrich stood in the fading light, hitting languid, low, easy-looking drives, resigned to her fate.

"Marlene looked great today," said Pavlova. "I was lucky to get on top of her."

"That reminds me," said Dietrich. "Is JFK here yet?"

"I'll come with you," said Tallulah Bankhead.

Day 9

Russell v. Dufy • Betjeman v. Bacon • Chaplin v. Le Corbusier • Keynes v. Ribeiro • Nabokov v. Miller • Conrad v. Graves • Rand v. Potter

In a big day for the Brits, Little Bertie Russell scampered through to the second round at the expense of well-supported local boy Raoul Dufy, losing concentration only once when confused by a call from the umpire overruling the baseline judge. The ball was called "out." The central umpire called it good and gave the point to Dufy.

"Pardon?" said Russell.

"I thought it was on the line," said the umpire.

"Where?" said Russell urgently, scanning the packed stand.

"The ball was good," said the umpire.

"The ball?" said Russell, interested. "Can a ball be 'good'?"

"On the line is good."

"Where?" said Russell, fiddling with his trousers.

English selectors were also pleased with the performance of John Betjeman, up against Francis Bacon, one of the youngest players here and a huge talent, if a bit unruly. "Oh, lovely play in the afternoon sun," said Betjeman as he put one across court. "Racquet head up, hit through the ball, John. Well done. Lemonade soon. Feel it in those thigh muscles."

"What's that?" asked Bacon.

"Sorry, talking to myself," said Betjeman.

"Thighs?" said Bacon.

And on Centre Court one of the few Englishmen openly adored by the French, Charles Chaplin, had an impressive win over Swiss-born French Davis Cup stalwart and veteran international Le Corbusier. When play started the partisan sections of the crowd began chanting their support for Corbu at one end and Charlot at the other. Corbu took the first set 6–3.

Initially nothing went right for Chaplin. Several times he turned himself over on the net, losing his racquet in the air and finishing on the ground on his opponent's side of the net facing the wrong way. At 3–4 and 0–30 in the second set he upset the drinks station and brought a container of iced beverages down on his head. At later stages of the match his trousers fell down, often as he was reaching for difficult overheads. "Charlot! Charlot!

Charlot!" called the crowd as he grabbed the second and third sets 7–5, 6–3. Corbu won the fourth but the little man came back and took the fifth to a standing ovation. Roses were tossed on to the court.

England's Maynard Keynes took an unusual tack on Court 6 this afternoon in his match with the very talented Portuguese lefty Aquilino Ribeiro. It annoyed Ribeiro that the Portuguese royal family was allocated one entire section at the southern end. "There are people out there who've been told there's no seating available," he said, "and we've got some pomaded ape up here with the best view in the house. He's been given thirty tickets! He only needs two! Let the people outside have the rest."

"I quite agree. Wait here," said Keynes, who went in search of the match referee.

"They should be gassed like badgers," said Ribeiro quietly when Keynes came back.

"I don't think that will be necessary."

As they watched, the king of Portugal was joined by a row of French peasants whose arrival was applauded by all and sundry.

"How did you do that?" asked Ribeiro.

"I bought the other seats from him and sold them to the peasants."

"They haven't got any money."

"They have now," said Keynes.

"Where did they get it?"

"I convinced the king to lend it to them."

"Why should he do that?" asked Ribeiro.

"He owns the drinks franchise, his company makes the hats and he prints the programs," said Keynes.

"How do you know that?"

"I went to school with him," said Keynes.

It wasn't all England today. Vladimir Nabokov, now resident in the US, derailed the comeback of Henry Miller, who has been out of the game with a socially sustained back injury and just seemed to be coming right. As Miller put it, "I hunt. I kill. I eat."

Nabokov has been playing since childhood in Russia, and can do almost anything with the ball on any surface. "I don't need to play tennis," he said. "I do it because it pleases me."

Miller seemed disappointed to have lost to "an elitist and a ponce" and, asked what he planned for the future, said he wanted to play with his instinct, not his brain.

"Unfortunately, there is a lot of this about," said Nabokov. "The idea that instinct is more radical than intellect is not one we need consider for long. Any other questions?"

Sixth-seed Joseph Conrad was fast and mobile against the baby-faced Robert Graves and he dealt well with swirling winds, and two interruptions while dead and dying insects were swept from the court. "I don't know what they were," said Conrad. "It was like a plague of some sort. A sickness."

Conrad didn't pick up a racquet until he was twenty-three and was the oldest player in the first tournament he entered. He won and never looked back. "It was good to be out there," he said. "I enjoyed it, apart from the horror." The Poles, of course, went mad.

Italian Maria Montessori went through comfortably and then invited the ballgirls out on to the practice courts for a hit. "They should play, all these children. Let them play and get confident and then they'll be better at everything they do."

"Silly bitch," said Ezra Pound. "She doesn't know what she's talking about. She doesn't speak for Italy."

"Ezra Pound is not Italian," said Montessori, "knows nothing about children, does not care about anyone but himself and is mad. Is there anything else?"

American glamour girl Gloria Swanson was also through today but perhaps the most emphatic win was Ayn Rand's annihilation of Beatrix Potter. Rand was brought up in Russia but lives now in the US where she thrives on the lucrative American circuit. She will appear before a hearing tomorrow night over an incident following the toss. The players shook hands. "Good luck, Ayn," said Potter.

"Get out of my way," replied Rand, "or I'll fucking kill you."

Day 10

Keaton v. Tzara • Spock v. Rivera • Lawrence v. Modigliani • Bishop v. Arden • McCarthy v. Doolittle • Ravel v. Hesse • Cocteau v. De Mille • Eliot v. Capek

The diminutive Buster Keaton endured everything thrown at him by Romanian Tristan Tzara. In the first-set tie-break a lighting tower crashed onto the court, missing him by centimeters. He stepped neatly out of the rubble as if it wasn't there.

Also solid was American qualifier Ben Spock, outlasting the Colombian José Rivera in 105-degree heat on Court 12 this afternoon. Conditions were so oppressive the match referee considered a postponement. "It was like playing in the jungle," said Rivera, "without any of the advantages."

An Olympic gold medalist in rowing, the Spockster was full of praise for his opponent. "José is a great player and he comes from a country which has been exploited and ruined by other countries, including my own. How can we bring children into the world and then do that to them?"

Lawrence of Nottingham marshaled his considerable will against the more fancied Amedeo Modigliani in the cauldron that was Court 4 this afternoon. The Italian beanpole was elegance personified and he began with some of the most imperious ground strokes we've seen here. He didn't even look where the ball had gone but nodded in quiet approval and strolled to his position to play the next point.

By contrast, Lawrence is like a young bull. He snorts. He grunts as he hits the ball and in today's heat he sweated, he groaned, he squinted, he poured water over himself in the breaks, he was not in his element at all. "I'm going to keep coming at you, you know," he said after the first set. "I'm going to keep coming at you until I have you." Modigliani looked slightly affronted at this but said nothing. For the next three sets, however, this is exactly what Lawrence did.

There was an entertaining media call after the Elizabeth Bishop–Eve Arden and the Mary McCarthy–Hilda Doolittle matches, which finished at almost the same time on different courts; Bishop successful over Arden and McCarthy over Doolittle. All the players were at the press conference except Arden, who "wasn't quite ready yet." Doolittle opened her mouth a couple of times but ultimately said nothing. A woman who announced herself as Bryher spoke for her. Doolittle was a great talent, Bryher said, and had trained with Pound, to whom she was engaged, and with Freud, to whom she was indebted. She said they had both been to SuperTom's match earlier that day and had watched "with deep admiration." She explained that Doolittle would have to be leaving soon. Bryher described herself as "unbelievably rich."

Bishop and McCarthy were at college together and delighted to be here. "I'm delighted to be anywhere," said Bishop. "Except New England and the past."

"Me too," said McCarthy. "The past can go to hell. Bring on the future."

"Yep," said Bishop, "and South America."

"Did anyone see the Lillian Hellman story in the paper today?" asked McCarthy. "Where she says she went into Germany and helped some people who were in trouble and then came back out again? What bullshit. She's sold the idea to some film producer. They're going to make a movie of it. Some pal of Dash's, no doubt."

"I read that," said Bishop. "Is it incorrect?"

"Absolute bullshit," insisted McCarthy. "Lillian's never been to Germany."

Chances are there'll be a good crowd for McCarthy's next singles match. Her opponent will be Lillian Hellman.

French Davis Cup regular Maurice Ravel came out with guns

blazing against the German Hermann Hesse, building up a rhythm, layer upon layer. Hesse was never in the first set and could do little but watch and wait, making Ravel fight for the points the gods didn't give him. He won his first game at 0–3 in the second set and glanced at the sky as if his call had been on hold but was now through. The crowd laughed but Ravel lost his way and began repeating the pattern of each point. Hesse simply put the ball where Ravel wasn't. Like Mann, Hesse attracts support from young American college students. They were out in force last night.

Last night, too, the brilliant Frenchman Jean Cocteau was pitted against the American powerhouse with the French name, Cecil B. De Mille. The match was preceded by a dispute about the lights. De Mille wanted all the lights on, Cocteau wanted half of them on and the area where the players sit between sets to be completely unlit.

"Unlit?" asked De Mille. "Why? How are we going to see what we're doing?"

"There's enough light spilling in from the court. It'll be great. Some contrast," said Cocteau.

"Contrast?" said De Mille. "People don't want contrast. They want to see what's going on."

"You don't know what people want. You only know what you want to give them," said Cocteau.

"Meaningless distinction," said De Mille. "Just turn the lights on so we can see."

The lights were turned on and play commenced. Cocteau spent much of the first set angling shots into De Mille from well above the net so they came at him out of the lights and he couldn't see a thing. De Mille complained to the umpire, who agreed, dismissing Cocteau's protest that the lights were De Mille's idea. Cocteau smiled. It was not the result that mattered, but the mischief.

De Mille plays well but lacks variation and, as the match progressed, his style became more metronomic, and the inventive Cocteau began to pick him off. De Mille had to be content with having executed, by his own estimation, at 4 all and 30–15 in the third set, "The Greatest Shot Ever Played in World Tennis." It wasn't enough.

There were no problems for the London-based SuperTom Eliot who was devastating against the resourceful Czech Karel Capek, sharpening his skills and hitting the ball as hard as anyone in the tournament so far. He has a bagful of racquets, each strung to a different tension and he worked his way through to the last of them.

"Just trying a few things," he said. The hangdog SuperTom recently gave up his bank job to devote himself to the tour full-time and has been practicing in the country with Ezra Pound. "Just a few little things we're working on," said Eliot.

"Can you be more specific?" he was asked.

"More specific?" interrupted Pound. "How could he be *more* specific?"

"It's all right, Ezra," said SuperTom and cleared his throat:

"*Légerdemain, Marie, c'est la!*
The second was the toughest set. A rugged time I had of it.
Après-dîner. Just the worst time for a match, and such a long *dîner*.
Because I did not serve too well.
Because I did not serve.
Because I did not serve my purpose
Was not clear *Meine Heimat über alles.*
I think those are *meine Tennisbälle.*
And timing please hurry along my timing.
The return is within the serve without the frame between.
Da."

Day 11

Puccini v. Shostakovich • Gaudier-Brzeska v. Sibelius • Epstein v. O'Casey • Kafka v. D'Annunzio • Stravinsky v. Rivera

Rain failed to dampen enthusiasm this morning and, if anything, was good for the seeds. Several of the courts became unplayable but by late afternoon showers were intermittent and meteorologists promise bluer skies tomorrow.

On Court 1, before the rains came, Giacomo Puccini looked good all the way over one-time Russian junior champion Dmitri Shostakovich, who did not appear happy when he was whisked away by Russian officials after the match. A worried Puccini said the Russian tennis program seemed to be designed to identify "an incomparable talent like Dmitri. And snuff it out."

Henri Gaudier-Brzeska found his road barred by the hardworking Finn Jean Sibelius. The Frenchman threw everything at it. Sibelius plays like no other player. "I play like a Finn," he said. "I am a Finn," he added, not unreasonably. His strokemaking sometimes seems agricultural, his serve lacks kick and he hits the ball straight and flat. The problem for his opponent today was that he hit it early and he hit it fast and he hit it into the gaps.

Englishman Jacob Epstein was also on the phone to the travel agent, beaten in four by Sean O'Casey. Epstein seems to have every shot but on the big points was tentative and sadly double-faulted to lose the match. O'Casey is a tough customer and his questioning of line calls brought him into conflict with the umpire. At 30–0 and 3–4 in the third set he did it again.

"You are questioning a number of line calls," said the umpire.

"I am," said O'Casey, "yes."

"Well, I wish you wouldn't."

"Do you think I'm doing it for the good of my health?" O'Casey asked. "I'm nearly blind, you great bollocks. I'm doing it because I can't see whether the fucking ball is in or out."

"The ball was out," said the umpire.

"Well, it didn't look out to me. Did you see it, Jacob?"

"No, I'm sorry, I didn't," said Epstein, "but I think we should accept the call."

"Oh, do you?" said O'Casey. "Think you're being conservative enough there, Jacob?"

"Thirty seconds," said the umpire.

"What's this thirty seconds business?" asked O'Casey.

"You have thirty seconds left or you'll incur a time penalty."

"You tosser," said O'Casey.

"Mr. O'Casey to serve," said the umpire.

"Tosser."

"Time penalty, Mr. O'Casey. 30–15."

"You're a tosser," said O'Casey.

"Time penalty, Mr. O'Casey. 30–all."

"Christ, you're playing a lot better now, Jacob."

"Time penalty, Mr. O'Casey. 30–40."

"Here, have a serve, man," said O'Casey, patting the balls toward Epstein. "Give the crowd something to look at."

"Game, Mr. Epstein," said the umpire.

"Up your arse," said O'Casey.

In the end, it didn't matter.

Franz Kafka is technically Czech although very much a German player in style and training. Consistently refused entry to the Czech national championships, he is still to play a tournament in his native Prague. There have been suggestions in recent events that his father is somehow communicating with him on court. "No one knows how they're doing it," said an opponent, "and certainly no one can prove it but, if his father is not there, K starts spraying his serve all over the place and his game falls apart."

Very much a loner off the court, Kafka has been romantically linked with two young women, but refuses to comment on marriage plans. "That is not the question," he said.

In his first appearance on Centre Court today, Kafka came up against the flamboyant Italian Gabriele D'Annunzio in an unusual match which sometimes descended into farce. D'Annunzio grabbed an early lead and then, at 2–2 in the second set when it looked as if there would be a rain interruption, began packing his bag—but Kafka came back out and stood waiting to receive service. D'Annunzio pointed to the service line where drops of rain were falling. The umpire asked Kafka what he thought. Kafka shrugged and referred the umpire to the tournament rules. This became the subject of some discussion between the umpire and the referee, Charles Darwin, who decided that play should continue. Back came D'Annunzio, singularly unimpressed, and prepared to serve. Kafka now drew the attention of the umpire to a sodden area of the court. The adaptable Darwin was called back, another regulation was cited by Kafka and play was halted.

D'Annunzio was very annoyed. "How can it be dry one minute and wet the next?" he asked.

"By reason of the effluxion of time," said Kafka.

"What on earth are we supposed to do? Man is a creature of action. We should be doing something."

"We are doing something."

"What are we doing?" asked D'Annunzio.

"We are waiting."

Day 12

Garbo v. Arendt • Pasternak v. Miró • Beiderbecke v. Malraux • Eisenstein v. O'Neill • Porter v. Borges • Faulkner v. Ray • Breton v. Isherwood

Greta Garbo, one of the most celebrated players in the history of the game, is out. She was on a plane this afternoon and we will not see her again. Seeded eighth, the Swedish ice maiden, born Greta Gustafsson and now living in the US, departed in style and issued a statement following her match with German American Hannah Arendt.

"I congratulate Hannah," the statement began. "She played most beautifully today and she deserved to win. I said before the tournament I would not be playing doubles with John Gilbert

"I mean something active. Man is supposed to be active. To have women. To fight."

"We are doing something active," said Kafka.

"What are we doing?" said D'Annunzio.

"We are avoiding having women or fighting," said Kafka.

When they came back the Italian took up where he left off until Kafka pulled out four blistering returns of service to change the course of the set and the match.

The big Italian was as surprised as his supporters when it was over. "I didn't do anything wrong," he said.

"I didn't do anything wrong either," said Kafka.

Igor Stravinsky was very much on song against Diego Rivera. The lumbering Mexican got his game working in the third set but by then the writing was on the wall. A bandaged woman in a richly colored dress shouted encouragement to him throughout the match but eventually he asked for her to be removed. He was warned twice for racquet abuse, three times for audible obscenities and once for indecent exposure.

or with Mercedes da Costa. I am a singles player. That is my condition. Good-bye."

This has been a shock. No one can believe it. "Garbo gone?" a man said. "Garbo? Gone where?"

"Huge surprise," said Arendt. "I can't remember a time when she wasn't at the very top."

And how did Arendt rate her own performance today?

"I think she let me play well," said Arendt.

Let you play well? Why would she do that?

"I think she wanted to go."

Let us get this straight. Greta Garbo threw her match?

"She didn't throw her match. That's your expression. I just think she wanted to go."

Big Boris Pasternak, carrying the hopes of Russia, ran away with his match against the Spaniard Joan Miró, who succeeded only in providing a track for the unstoppable Pasternak train. Pasternak is another player at odds with his own national administrators, and questions must be asked about whether those entrusted with the organization of the code in Russia are fully possessed of the facts. Pasternak is power personified. He hit the ball today with such force and depth it is difficult to imagine how an opponent might approach the question of resistance. His victory, when it came, was treated by the huge crowd as the final chord in a great symphony. It met the requirements of drama, of music and of history.

Two days ago Bix Beiderbecke was backed in from 100–1 to

4–1. It is difficult to say what went wrong. André Malraux was generous in victory. "I didn't think I had any chance," he said. "The Americans are just so strong. My only plan was to try to upset his rhythm." To be fair, Malraux is a very experienced campaigner, having won in France, China, Spain and Britain. Once banned from the German Open, he turned up under an assumed identity and won. Today he cramped Beiderbecke and put him under the hammer from the outset. Some of his cross-court passing shots were glorious.

"I wasn't overconfident," Beiderbecke said. "I didn't serve badly. I made very few unforced errors. Plain fact is, the guy was too good."

A four-hour battle was waged on Court 1 late yesterday between Russian Sergei Eisenstein and American Eugene O'Neill. O'Neill had seventeen match points and Eisenstein twelve before the weary Russian nudged a return just beyond the reach of a desperate O'Neill lunge. It was nearly ten o'clock, the air was full of fireflies and the crowd rose as the players embraced and departed, sure in the knowledge that Thermopylae was safe. When the final score was dispatched, the wire services were obliged to send confirmation three times.

Eisenstein has a day to recover before again stepping up to the plate. "And I'll need it," he said. "I got so tired at one stage I looked up at the crowd in the terraces and they seemed to be moving, running up and down the steps, there were women, old men, children, there was a pram."

"I had a similar experience," said O'Neill, "only everyone up there was my father."

Cole Porter is one of the few Americans here who hits a single-handed backhand and uses a racquet with a wooden frame. He has no sponsorship and seeks none. "Sponsors' clothing is hideous and their intentions are dishonorable in the extreme," he explained. He describes himself as an amateur professional. "I don't do this for a living," he said. "I play only for money." His consistent, elegant tennis today overwhelmed the Argentinian Jorge Borges, who couldn't see how he could lose.

Borges has won his own national championship a record fifteen times, has always performed well in Europe and has all the shots. "There are two types of Borges," said Borges. "The one who divides everything up into two parts, and the one who doesn't. It is sometimes difficult to know which one I am being. I don't, for example, know which of the two is making this statement."

Two other Americans with strong French connections, real or imagined, were up against each other today when Bill Faulkner, "from Jefferson County, Mississippi, get that down, not America, Mississippi," met Man Ray, whose years in Philadelphia were followed by a lengthy period in Paris, honing new techniques. Ray has many friends here and in some respects is quite a French player. An image of him at the French Open two years ago at the northern end of the court in the late afternoon, outlined in shadow and flicking a gorgeous drive past his opponent, is still posted on the tournament's website. Faulkner says he was also here as a younger player, with a Canadian air force team, although there is no record of any Faulkner in the Canadian squad during the period. Ray played some exquisite tennis but Faulkner simply outlasted him.

"I didn't outlast him," he said later. "I beat him."

André Breton was beaten in five by the rapidly improving Christopher Isherwood, one of the few English players at this event who has never cracked a Davis Cup berth. "I don't know why," he said. "I live in LA, I'm a gay Hindu. I can't think what might be holding me back." One thing is for sure. It won't be his tennis.

Day 13

Heidegger v. Marx • Chesterton v. Auden •
Rushdie v. Pound • Orwell v. Arlen

The first-round men's matches were all completed today, roughly on schedule after some were moved to outside courts to make up time lost to rain delays.

When it comes to power serving, German Martin Heidegger is a benchmark. He has a huge shoulder turn and generates enormous height on his action. Drawn against American Groucho Marx, he peeled off a succession of aces to the obvious satisfaction of German administrators. Not much is known about Marx but late in the second set he began to pick the Heidegger serve early and hit it on the up. By the third set Marx was running around his backhand. By the fourth set he was running around his accountant. He was trying to get his accountant to run around his backhand when the match finished. Heidegger was furious and said he thought he was being mocked.

"Smart fellow," said Groucho. "Pity we won't be seeing more of him."

The very dextrous Englishman Gilbert Chesterton, in the twilight of his career now, gave his countryman Wystan Auden the mother of all surprises on Court 4 this afternoon. He guessed that his best chance against Auden was to come out with his britches on fire. It very nearly worked but Auden is a volume and through-put man and, once he gets his eye in, big Wystan can hit the ball all day. At 2–5 in the third he came out smoking.

"The way he understood the match rather than the games was interesting," Chesterton said. "I haven't seen that before. Most players will get upset if they lose a lot of games. Auden had a much better sense of the match than I did."

A hastily organized exhibition match between Salman Rushdie and Ezra Pound, planned for tonight and set up as a showcase for a prodigious young talent and one of the great masters of the modern game, has had to be postponed. Pound is openly reviled by many players for remarks he made on Italian radio, although the real problem is the threat from an unnamed group believed to be based in Morocco to "take out the entire stadium" if any match involving Rushdie is broadcast on network television. Pound rejected a proposal to stage the fixture at another venue.

"I'm not playing in a false beard on some up-country cow paddock just because this guy can't keep his mouth shut," said Pound. "You people couldn't organize a shit. In Germany they'd fill the joint stiff with uniformed police, play the match and anyone who doesn't like it gets a faceful of footwear."

"I don't think that's altogether consistent of him," said Rushdie. "He's hardly in a position to lecture others on how to keep their mouths shut. He'd have been rubbed out long ago if he hadn't pleaded insanity, which, if I might assay a purely personal opinion, he's in a very good position to do."

"It's a terrible shame," said Nike supremo Nietzsche. "It looks like being one of the great grudge matches. I'm going to be there, wherever it is."

And would he care to pick a winner?

"Too hard. It depends on who is faster. And who is fitter, I think," he added.

"Who is younger," said the quietly confident Rushdie.

"Who is silvier," said Pound, obliquely.

George Orwell, or "the artist formerly known as Eric Blair" as he is sometimes called by the other players, beat American Harold Arlen in straight sets. Arlen played well but Orwell had too much.

"Too good," said Arlen. "I tried to accentuate the positive but it was pretty stormy weather and I couldn't get happy. Round and round I go, down and down I go, I don't know. Somewhere, over the rainbow . . . what are you writing, George?"

Orwell looked up. "Pardon? Oh nothing. Just a children's story I'm fiddling with. Sorry, what were you saying?"

"Read it out," said Arlen. "What is it?"

"It's just a story," said Orwell.

"Go on," said Arlen. "Let's hear it."

"Once upon a time there was a puppy called Ma," Orwell read, "and he had an idea of how to make everything in the world work nicely.

" 'Nice world,' said Ma.

"When Ma grew up into a big dog he understood that there were other dogs who didn't agree with him. They wanted the world to be a bad place. So Ma bit them until they died. He thought his idea was better because it had a better name.

" 'Nice world,' said dog Ma."

"Read it again, George," said Arlen.

Round 2

Day 14

Chekhov v. Grainger • Proust v. Klee • Munch v. Betjeman • Stopes v. Besant • Baker v. Goncharova • Satie v. Carnap • Gershwin v. Segovia • Chaplin v. Carmichael • Hardy v. Koestler • Steinbeck v. Waugh

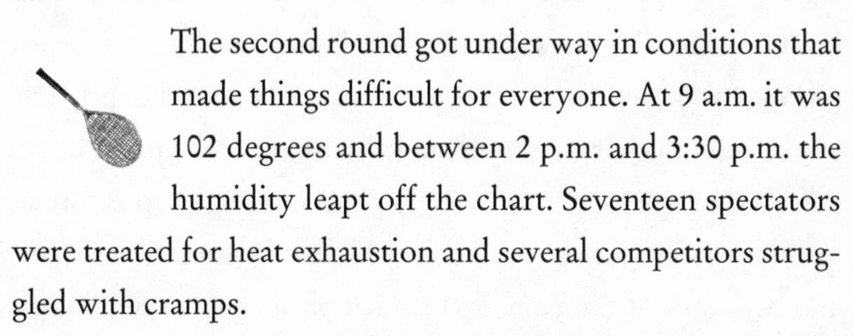

The second round got under way in conditions that made things difficult for everyone. At 9 a.m. it was 102 degrees and between 2 p.m. and 3:30 p.m. the humidity leapt off the chart. Seventeen spectators were treated for heat exhaustion and several competitors struggled with cramps.

The players did what they could and some did it better than others. Top seed Chekhov was not inconvenienced by a spectacular display of ball-striking from gifted Australian qualifier Percy Grainger, who didn't mind being beaten. Had he got his first serve in more consistently he might have stolen the opening set but Chekhov, who has been saying in press conferences all week that he wants to go to Moscow, is a model of concentration. In fact, it is beginning to look as if his public statements may not be entirely serious. After today's match, for example, he practiced for two hours and then said, "There's nothing to do here. I want to go to Moscow."

As the temperature rose there was every chance the first casualty of the heat might be Marcel Proust, who looked to be struggling even during the hit-up.

"I was," he said later, "conscious, in that way in which an awareness exists of some sense in which the recalled and the recalling are drawn together to coexist in time, but which also remain distinct, each from the other, perfect and imperfect, fixed and drifting, oppressive and liberating, that the day before, when I had left the practice courts and walked across the park, I had been distracted by the water, not in its liquid movement or depth or color so much as by the way its movement and depth and color were forged into something else by the alchemy of being absorbed by my gaze, undirected as it was by any purpose, formal or otherwise, or any force of which I knew, beyond a sensitivity and perhaps not even a particular sensitivity but a mingling of perception and instinct which was acting not just upon me but on everyone who saw it, or who saw anything else."

The lanky Parisian can never be written off. He has got to the quarters in an unbroken run of sixteen French Opens and you don't do that by accident. On the other hand he has been doing a lot of his training "lying down." His first thought this morning was that he might have to withdraw from his match against Paul Klee. "He is not strong enough," said the French team doctor. "His respiratory system cannot bear the strain."

"I will play," said Proust eventually. "I have come here to play and I will play."

Results of tests should be known later tonight but it is believed the problem may be traceable to some pastries he consumed at breakfast.

Proust did just enough to go through, albeit under what must be one of the biggest injury clouds in living memory.

If Proust thought he had problems in the heat he might have spared a thought for Norwegian wraith Eddie Munch, who returned to Paris only this morning from an overnight trip to Oslo occasioned by a family bereavement. He traveled straight to the stadium for his match with John Betjeman and, as he said, "I caught sight of myself in a window as we came out on court and I looked shithouse. I looked at the thermometer, which said 105°F. I looked at Betjeman, who said, 'Lovely day for it' and I thought, 'Oh God! why do I keep doing this?'"

At the beginning of the second set he was officially informed by Charles Darwin that his father was dangerously ill. The remainder of the match was played in a somber atmosphere and Munch left for Norway the moment it concluded, after first thanking Betjeman for his kind understanding.

"Terribly difficult for poor Munch," said Betjeman. "I remember my own father's death. One feels so much a disappointment to them, especially with one's not wanting to take over the family firm, and one thing and another."

By the time Marie Stopes and Annie Besant emerged from the players' race the temperature on the ground at Centre Court was 114 degrees. Besant, the oldest competitor in the women's draw, has plenty of experience in oppressive conditions but from the outset the Scottish Stopes handled them better.

"Sometimes when the balls get very hot," she said, "they can swell slightly and come on to you a lot faster. What I tried to do today was get in and put them away at the net."

Also good in the heat were Daisy Bates, who grew up playing in Australia and only took her cardigan off at 2–2 in the second set, and Josephine Baker, who romped through her match against Russian icon Goncharova and then went for "a light run."

French hopes were raised today when local prodigy Eric Satie hit his straps against Rudolf Carnap.

The thoughtful German looked sharp early, hitting the ball crisply and playing to a plan. Satie, however, is no mean strategist himself and doesn't seem to mind who he's playing. "In this caper," he said, "you're really playing yourself, although this process is influenced by how others are playing."

Carnap worked on his timing and space and kept Satie on the run in the heat. Satie did the opposite and just about drove Carnap mad, returning the ball again and again to the same point. Carnap would move, preparing himself, waiting for the inevitable change in the routine. Then back would come another shot, exactly the same.

"It's not actually the same shot," Satie explained. "Some are hard, some are soft, some have topspin, some have backspin, some float. And the context changes; the ninth is different from the first. It looks the same but it isn't. It's the ninth."

Ira Gershwin was over the moon in the media tent this afternoon. "S'wonderful," he said. "Strike up the band." Brother George, with whom he's playing in the doubles, had just fought his way back from two sets down and 0–4 to get up and beat the brilliant Catalonian Andrés Segovia. Inspired by the performance of his compatriots Waller, Armstrong and Ellington this week, George has been practicing with them, enjoying his game more and playing more in their style. Segovia is an elegant player and has remarkable hands. Time and again he hit what looked like drives deep to the back corners but at the last minute he rolled his wrists over and they became drop shots of the greatest delicacy. In the end, however, it was Gershwin's new style of play and sheer persistence which got him over the line.

In the most entertaining match of the day the popular Charlot had a win over Hoagland Carmichael. Carmichael's serve lacked control, especially with Chaplin dancing around it and banging it back at his ankles as he followed it in. "Charlie's got everything worked out," he explained, "but he makes it all look so simple you want to reach out and pat him on the head."

As Chaplin attempted to leave the media conference, a camera crew barged through the door and pinned him against the wall. When the door swung back he fell flat on the floor. An official came in and Chaplin rather surprisingly kicked him firmly in the seat of the pants and fell over again. When the official turned around Chaplin was lying on the floor. The official took a swing at Hoagy, who had bent over to help Chaplin, and belted the concrete wall instead. Chaplin stood up, kicked the official in the pants again and fell over. This happened four times. The official finally realized it was Chaplin who was kicking him and chased him around a table at high speed until Chaplin opened the door and the hapless official hurtled back out into the main concourse and sprinted into a display of oranges.

This joyous mood did not survive the Thomas Hardy–Arthur Koestler match. Hardy once again clashed with officials over the treatment of the waitressing staff, one of whom became distressed when Koestler claimed she was making too much noise. Hardy protested that this was unfair. "If she goes, I go," he said.

After an in-camera hearing, during which Hardy kept the crowd in their seats with some haunting stories, it was revealed that Koestler will be questioned about a number of incidents involving other young women. A sobering and most unexpected development.

The night match featured the hardworking John Steinbeck coming home to take the points in an all-out scrap with England's Evelyn Waugh.

"Dreadful oik," Waugh said. "Americans are of two kinds. The rich and more moronic type of show-off and the poor, many of whom are racially disadvantaged or insane. Dreadful oiks with German names fall into the latter class but with pretensions to the former."

Steinbeck, clearly irritated, rallied in the third set. He upped the volume on his serve and hit the ball from both sides with great ferocity. Waugh seemed to lose his touch and his unforced errors gave the fifth set to the American.

"Waugh imagines he's quite a character," said Steinbeck. "But there are kids out there watching who've got no money and think they've got no chance of playing this game. I wanted to show them that they have. It's a hell of a fight. But they can do it."

There was a minor sensation late this evening when French journalist Roland Barthes was asked to step into the Committee Room, where a heated exchange took place concerning his comment in Thursday's edition of *Paris-Match*. Barthes contended that the game has undergone such fundamental change that the relationship between the commentators and the crowd is now the principal intellectual contract. In effect, he said, the player is dead.

Sources say discussions with the chairman of the committee reached an impasse when Barthes was asked whether his comments were in the nature of a personal opinion. He observed that, since he was a writer employed to report on the game, his personal opinion was also going to become the personal opinion of many other people.

The chairman advanced the view that, if the age of the player was over, Mr. Barthes could spare himself the trouble of attending the remainder of the tournament.

Barthes replied that, since the discussion of the event was more important than the event itself, it was immaterial whether he attended it or not. The significant thing would be what he wrote about it.

"You won't be able to write much about it if you don't see it, will you, sunshine?" said the chairman.

"You obviously don't know anything about the game's history," retorted Barthes.

"It is precisely because of my knowledge of such matters," said the chairman, "that I have been entrusted with the chairmanship."

"How can you possibly have witnessed *everything* that has happened since the inception of the game?"

"I didn't say I'd witnessed it. You asked me if I knew about it."

"You've read about it?"

"Of course I've bloody read about it."

Barthes smiled. "No further questions, your honor," he said.

"Mr. Barthes," said the chairman, "please understand that you have no further accreditation at this event, and will be refused entry to all remaining matches."

"I'm not interested in attendance. I'm concerned with symbols and signifiers," said Barthes.

"If attendance is not the point," asked the chairman, "where are you going to get a crowd from?"

"The crowd is a function of the commentary, not of the game," said Barthes. "The better the commentator, the better the crowd."

"Your crowd wouldn't fill a phone booth, Roland. They're a bunch of seed-spillers who wouldn't know if you were up them with an armful of chairs. Without the game none of you would exist. You want to wake up to yourself, son."

"We sell more copies of *Paris-Match* than you do of the official program," said Barthes. "You're out of touch, pal. People are much more absorbed by what it all signifies than they are by what actually happened."

"And what does it all signify, as a matter of interest?"

"Not telling," said Barthes. "Buy the magazine."

Day 15

Muir v. Toulouse-Lautrec • Huxley v. Robeson • Wodehouse v. Chagall • Wells v. Hearn • West v. Stead • Bankhead v. Smith • Arendt v. Beach • Wittgenstein v. Lawrence • Nijinsky v. Hartley • Spock v. Diaghilev • Seurat v. Ernst • Wright v. Rilke • Derain v. Prevert

Last night world rankings were tossed in the air and fancied players treated to some of the rudest awakenings on record. Toulouse-Lautrec, Chagall, Lawrence, Diaghilev, Lloyd Wright and Ernst are all out of the men's draw. West, Beach and Bankhead were toppled in the women's.

Le Monde carried a large front-page photograph this morning of Edwin Muir in a tam-o'-shanter being congratulated by popular night owl Henri Toulouse-Lautrec after their match, under the headline, SCOT THE WHOLE WORLD IN

HIS HANDS. French officials were furious. They felt Lautrec had "wasted his chances," had been "very silly and a show-off."

Great deeds continued to mount as the bookies' nightmare deepened. Aldous Huxley's pedigree includes a good portion of the studbook in his native England. Brothers Julian and Andrew and grandfather T. H. all have their names etched on the British championship and he is ranked seventy places above the man who beat him, the American Paul Robeson. "Paul's good," said Huxley, pouring balm into his own wounds. "He's a big man and he hits the ball hard but he can also hit it softly. You can prepare for the power stuff because you expect it. It's the gentle stuff that gets you."

"Aldous wasn't seeing it well," said Robeson, "but he played beautifully. I enjoyed the match. The Welsh were there, the Russians, the Africans and Asians. The only ones missing were the American Davis Cup selectors."

Completing the night's revels was Plum Wodehouse, whose opponent, the illustrious Russian Marc Chagall, has become almost synonymous with French tennis. Chagall flew through the first set but then tired and even had a little lie down at the top of the court. His other problem was Wodehouse, whose return of service was deadly. "It had to be," he said. "Friend Chagall climbs all over his first serve and if I hadn't had a rigorous workout recently from a particularly helpful aunt, it may well have been curtains."

On Court 4 this afternoon the Herbie Wells–Lafcadio Hearn match was in progress. Sitting at courtside was Wells' mixed-doubles partner Rebecca West. It was clear from the way Wells glared at her between points that her comments were increasingly unsettling him.

"Will you be quiet, please?" he asked her at 6–3 and 3–0. "I know what I'm doing. Look at the board. I'm 6–3 and 3–0."

"You'll lose," she said, and pulled her collar up.

Herbie appealed to have her removed but the umpire indicated there had been no actual offense.

"Would it help if *I* left?" asked Hearn, insistent on a gesture of some kind.

"She's talking while I'm trying to play," said Wells. "It's outrageous."

"I'm trying to help," said West.

"I don't need help," said Wells. "I'm winning."

"You'll lose," said West and pulled her collar higher.

"I don't think I can continue to play," said Wells.

"What *can* you continue to do?" asked West.

"Quiet, please," said the umpire. "Mr. Wells to serve."

"She's looking at me," said Herbie.

"Everyone's looking at you," said West. "Isn't that what you want?"

"The Japanese are a serene people, devoted to ritual," said Hearn. "They would have a way of dealing with this."

"No argument with that," conceded Wells. "We have much to learn from the medieval warlord cultures."

"The English, for example," said West.

"You really are a fraud," said Wells. "You're not in the least bit interested in the Irish cause."

"I don't have to be," said West. "I am Irish."

"Mr. Wells to serve," said the umpire. "Quiet, please."

Wells served. Hearn served. Wells served. In the fourth set he got so jumpy he sent down fifteen double faults. In the end he escaped 7–5.

"You're useless," said West.

"I won," said Herbie.

"Lucky," said West.

"I'm playing some of the best tennis of my life," he said.

"Who are you playing in the next round?"

"I don't know," said Wells.

"You'll lose," said West and turned away.

Elsewhere Frida Kahlo announced she would not play any further matches with partner Diego Rivera and requested assistance in removing a tattoo of Rivera from the middle of her forehead. And Peggy Guggenheim, who had insisted to officials that she and Beckett would play together, said Beckett knew nothing of this and she now wished to compete with Max Ernst.

Later this afternoon West herself was knocked out of the singles by the promising Australian Christina Stead, who offered West her support. "Rebecca was distracted out there today. I know something of what she's being put through. I'm sure most of us do."

West issued a statement saying she was returning to London and would not appear in the mixed.

"Typical Rebecca," said Wells. "Change your mind on the spur of the moment. No discussion. No consultation. Completely irrational."

"What an arsehole," said Stead.

"Rebecca's own son agrees with me," said Wells.

"And what sex is her son?" asked Stead. "Is he, for example, male?"

"The point is, what am I supposed to do now?"

"Of course," said Stead. "Of course that is the point."

Tallulah Bankhead, beaten by Bessie Smith, explained she was really here to play in the mixed but wasn't quite sure who would partner her. "Haven't decided yet. I'm looking."

Does she like what she sees?

"I do. Yes. Very much."

When does she think she'll know?

"Not sure. Auditions are coming along nicely."

Does she concede that this is all a little bit unusual?

"For whom, dear?"

Hannah Arendt, who beat Sylvia Beach today and looks very good, was in even worse trouble. She was asked if she could explain her choice of mixed-doubles partner.

"The question is flawed. Martin Heidegger is the partner I have chosen. No one else can make my choice."

That is acknowledged. But could she nevertheless please explain it?

"The fact that you do not understand something does not compel me to explain it."

How might it be possible to understand something without information?

"You did not ask for information or for understanding, but for an explanation."

Could she speak into the microphone, please?

"Certainly."

Has she known Heidegger for a long time?

"For many years."

And have they played together a lot?

"Many, many times."

How did she explain the fact that their games seemed so different?

"Could you put that question again without the word 'seem' in it?"

Would she not admit that Heidegger's entire approach was different from her own?

" 'Admit'? What is this? I'm not allowed to select my own partner?"

Could she answer the question, please?

"I suggest the person to ask about 'Heidegger's entire approach' is Heidegger."

But how might Heidegger's approach differ from her own?

"In that it is Heidegger's."

Did she agree with Heidegger?

"Heidegger believes we should go to dinner tonight. I am considering this."

Mystery man Ludwig Wittgenstein was matched against the combined might of the highly fancied Lawrence of Nottingham, his personal trainer Frieda, sister of the Red Baron, the entire British press and 3000 English supporters.

Frank "the Ferret" and Queenie Leavis, already eliminated, have been whipping up interest in the young champion. "There are five great players," the Ferret told Roland Barthes, "and Lawrence is one of only two still alive; the other of course being Jane Austen."

When it was pointed out that Austen had died in 1817, the Ferret took the view that "in that rather narrow and limited sense she is, certainly, not as fully alive within the conventional meaning of the term, as are, for example, a great many persons still living today."

Wittgenstein perked up somewhat when he heard this. "That is interesting," he said and for twenty minutes he remained silent. Then he said, "No."

The result of the match was never in doubt as Lawrence found himself bereft of any real defense against the deceptive angles and superb ground strokes of a top international player very much at the height of his powers. English bookmakers will have dropped a bundle today and Lawrence's first task when he returns home is to appear before a disciplinary hearing following an outburst in the first set which obliged officials to clear the court and disinfect the area behind the baseline at the southern end.

In other matches, Nijinsky brushed Les Hartley aside, Spock took Diaghilev apart and local fervor was satisfied by the passage of Georges Seurat through the challenging waters of the Bay of Ernst.

Nijinsky continues to look fabulous, although after the match he described himself as "The Supreme Being" and offered to describe how he created the world. Friends say this is not a good sign.

Diaghilev was shocked to go out of the tournament, especially to someone who has never won at this level, but the Spockster is fit and smart and read the match well. "Diaghilev sees this whole thing as a battle between men. He told me during the hit-up that he would crush me, so I knew he had a problem. He didn't need to crush me. He just needed to play better tennis."

"Mad" was Diaghilev's verdict on his opponent. "If I ever play him again I'll crush him."

The finale this evening had an element of tragedy about it. Frank Lloyd Wright, lackluster against John Masefield in the first round, came out tonight against Rainer Rilke with a different plan. "This time I went back to what I learned in Tokyo." (Wright won the Japanese Open the year the tournament was played during an earthquake.) Rilke won the first set and at 2–4 in the second Wright sat down and began to run water over his head and across his shoulders, allowing it to cascade over the back of the chair and onto the ground. At 4–4 he ran it down his arms and let it plunge from his thighs onto some nearby plants. Then he came out and began opening up huge spaces out wide and balancing them with volleys to the other side. In no time he had taken the second set and was looking a very good thing at 5–2 in the third. His confidence was high and he was punching the air and shouting "Come on!" after points which went his way.

The more assured Wright became of victory, however, the more Rilke lifted. At 8–8 in the tie-break Rilke dropped back and moved wide to receive service and Wright went down the middle. How Rilke got to this is anyone's guess but he put it on the line in the back corner. Wright knew he was in trouble at a set down and the Czech looked as if he had just invented a new type of saxophone. Wright came back and took the fourth and might have pulled off a famous victory if Rilke hadn't kept his head, steadied and got the job done.

André Derain, in easily the loudest shorts we've seen so far, looked a class above his compact countryman Jacques Prevert, but afterwards had little to say about his own form.

"Did you see Matisse?" he said. "What a player! Did you see him against Miller? What a match! He was magnificent. Six times I thought he was gone and he came back. There's only one man in the tournament who can beat him."

And who might that be?

"The Dutchman, van Gogh. I saw him play for the first time

just the other day. If that guy doesn't change the way this whole game is played I'm a monkey's uncle."

Derain has been asked to present himself to referee Charles Darwin, "for a few quiet words regarding trousers, predictions and primates generally."

Day 16

Earhart v. Luxemburg • Duncan v. Mandelstam • Christie v. Noether • McCarthy v. Hellman • Keynes v. Paderewski • Mayakovsky v. Porter • Gödel v. Hemingway • Pirandello v. Lacan

Today number 1 seed Amelia Earhart was knocked out. The marvelous Isadora Duncan was stretchered off. Agatha Christie went missing and French police hold "grave fears" for her safety. And just before the close of business Lillian Hellman launched legal proceedings against Mary McCarthy.

On top of everything else a submission has been put by a group representing "the players" that they should be able to enter the doubles with multiple partners.

Earhart's plan against Rosa Luxemburg was to rush the net

at every opportunity. With Luxemburg in a defiant mood, however, it was a plan that never got off the ground. Time and again she was passed as she came in. "Are you going to keep doing that all day?" she asked Luxemburg.

"I have to beat you to stay in the tournament," said Luxemburg. "We're in a cockfight. Let's just refuse to play against one another."

"If we refuse to play the tournament won't work."

"Exactly," said Luxemburg. "Then we can get the rules changed and start again without trying to eliminate one another."

"You mean change the way the whole system works?"

"Of course."

"I don't think so. Get back up there. I'm going to serve even faster."

"And I'm going to belt it back past you as you come in."

Both players were correct in these prognostications.

Two courts away the crowd was traumatized when Isadora Duncan caught part of her clothing in the umpire's stand as she stretched for a drop shot. There was a sickening thud as her head snapped back and she didn't move again. Her opponent Nadezhda Mandelstam was shaken and after the match was counseled by Russian officials by being forced to dig her own grave and stand next to it naked.

French police have issued a description of Agatha Christie and are stopping traffic in and out of the area. Christie was last seen two nights ago on a train with a Welsh male voice choir and an extension ladder. Her second-round match against the understanding Amalie Noether has been rescheduled for Friday.

Mary McCarthy was giving an interview after her win over Lillian Hellman this evening when she was handed a writ. "Good Lord," she said. "Hellman is suing me. What for?" Her eye ran down the document. "Listen to this: 'That McCarthy did allege both publicly and privately that Hellman did not compete in the German Open and did not win it in a heroic manner and that, further, Hellman had never been to Germany.'" McCarthy put the writ down and asked for a glass of water.

Would McCarthy be making a statement at some future time?

"McCarthy will be making a statement right now," she said. "Everything that Lillian Hellman says or writes is a lie, including 'and' and 'the.'"

After this the motion that competitors should be able to play doubles with multiple partners seemed tame. It was seconded by Peggy Guggenheim, Eleanor Roosevelt, Tallulah Bankhead, Edna St. Vincent Millay, and everyone in the men's draw except Auden.

From the beginning of his match against fluent and charismatic Jan Paderewski, John Keynes determined that one of the keys to winning this was to make his opponent play a lot of balls. "Padders has been hitting the ball so well this week," Keynes said later, "I couldn't let him just stand and deliver. The more winners he hit the more the marginal propensity for error increased and the more confidence I seemed to get in my own game, over time."

Betting markets responded by firming, with support for Nijinsky, Keynes and Picasso. The big mover was Spock, from 80s in to 7s.

An hour after Isadora Duncan's terrible accident there was another medical emergency, this time on Court 11. Vladimir Mayakovsky has been impressive here in practice and Cole Porter is playing the tennis of his life. Porter won the first set with a barrage of volleying and measured drop shots. The Russian came back in the second, varying his pace, slowing his serve down and moving Porter around more. At 3–3 in the third set a ball called "out" by the linesperson was overruled as "in" by the Austro-Hungarian umpire who then became concerned that he had upset Mayakovsky.

"No. I'm happy," said Mayakovsky.

"Play a let if you like," said the umpire.

"No. You're the boss," said Mayakovsky.

"You're the boss," agreed Porter, "you're the judge and jury."

"You're the boss," they assured him, "and you're both the Curies,

"You're the quick response, of the dog of old Pavlov,
You're the clout of Ruth, you're the hope of youth,
You're Ulyanov.

You're the grace of a novice kneeling,
You're the height of the Sistine ceiling,
You're a yard and a half of the Queen's Own Household Guards,

You're Atlantic flights, you're the Northern Lights,
You're credit cards.

You're the luft in the old luftwaffe,
You're the catch in a cash-back offer,
You're Revere's ride and you're vaudeville before it died.
You're the rebel yell, you're the Liberty Bell,
You're genocide.

You're the rise, in a great crescendo,
You're the fall, of diminuendo,
When the rolling stones have rolled, you are the moss,
And if we, sir, are the players, you're the boss."

And so it went, and a delightful spectacle it all was until Porter fell and twisted his back, damaging a leg so badly he had to be strapped and stretchered off.

Kurt Gödel was brilliant for two sets but couldn't go the distance against a hard-hitting Ernie Hemingway, who finished, dripping with sweat, bandages on his left arm and right knee and with a cut over his eye, looking like a gladiator, spent but victorious. Gödel said later that he proved what he had set out to prove and was happy. Asked what this was, he remarked that "it is difficult to prove anything."

"Crap," said Hemingway. "There was him and there was me. Two of us. The old one and the young one. In the sun. By the middle of the day it would be hot. We both knew what would happen. We would both sweat. Old sweat and young sweat. We both knew."

There appeared to be a scuffle in the crowd during Luigi Pirandello's confidence-building win over the young French pretender Jacques Lacan but police reported no trouble, just a half dozen characters who had turned up at the wrong venue. And in the best of the matches late in the day, Big Bill Yeats played the important points well against Fermi and was delighted to get out of a close contest with a lovely forehand crosscourt winner in the warm purple twilight of an evening dripping with promise.

Day 17

Sartre v. Mandelstam • Matisse v. Low • Apollinaire v. Benchley • Fields v. Dali • Montessori v. Markievicz • Pavlova v. Klein • Magritte v. Kazantzakis

It was 11:49 a.m. The French media were in disarray. The players had left the arena. The crowd was stunned. Jean-Paul Sartre had just been beaten. Gone. Good night nurse. *Eliminé*.

Some say he was lucky to get past Duke Ellington in the first round. French commentators disagreed. Everyone has a bad match somewhere in a tournament, they argued; Ellington was his and JPS would move on.

It looked like business as usual as the players warmed up. Sartre appeared to be moving well, hitting the ball hard and serving at full strength in front of a huge partisan crowd, many of them students.

But let us now praise famous Mandelstam, who was magnificent today. It is hard to think of a shot he didn't play and after 2–0 in the third he didn't lose a point.

Sartre's response after his demolition was to quarrel with Simone de Beauvoir over the idea of multiple partners in the mixed doubles.

"We disagree. I am opposed to the proposal in its current form. If I wish to have multiple partners I will do so. And so can de Beauvoir. Although if she does, I won't be one of them."

De Beauvoir's position is slightly different. "I support the right of all women to have multiple partners but since my man doesn't want me to do so, I will be doing as I'm told."

"I am a feminist too," said Sartre. "I support your right to do so."

"I have, however, played with other partners in the past," said de Beauvoir.

"You're telling me you have," said Nelson Algren from the players' box.

"But from now on I won't be doing that," continued de Beauvoir. "I will be writing about it."

"Heartless bitch," said Nelson Algren.

"Get the car, Simone," said Sartre. "We're leaving."

Strictly speaking this wasn't a great morning for French prestige. Henri Matisse spent nearly four hours trying to hold out New Zealander David Low before getting on top of him in the final set. Low made a lot of friends in this match and Matisse was impressed. He said afterwards it was the best match he had played in a long time and that Low was a considerable player whose influence on the game would be profound. "In England he has already changed the look of the game."

Next door on Court 3 local clay court specialist Billy Apollinaire found himself in a heap of trouble against the resourceful Robert Benchley, who had come to the match on his way back from dinner "at the home of someone called Harris." The American played the first set very gingerly, in a sweater and dark glasses and socks "to keep the noise down." Apollinaire grabbed the initiative in the third and was up 3–1 when Uncle Bob got annoyed by some pigeons sitting on the roof. He scowled at them. He walked over to them and explained the situation. "That's the thing with pigeons. They like clarity." He was prepared to be reasonable, he said. He was trying to get some work done and could they please be quiet, less "pigeonlike" and "could you three, in particular, stop looking askance at me?"

Apollinaire tried everything but Benchley got out of jail after the pigeons agreed to terms.

And will he be practicing his serve before his next match?

Benchley smiled. Yes, he said. He would. As soon as he could find Harris.

Another chapter of oddities began on the same court shortly afterwards when Bill Fields turned up at four o'clock to find he had no opponent, Salvador Dali having arrived an hour earlier on Court 4 to find that he, also, had no opponent. Both players were notified that their match would commence at 3 at 4. Officials explained that their intention was to start the match at four o'clock on Court 3.

If that was the case, the remarkable Spaniard asked, why had it been advertised on television as a feature match? He was only here to play in feature matches, he said, and the middle of the afternoon on a remote court was not a feature match. Fields felt that the match should be postponed for twenty-four hours. Dali agreed and suggested the matter be put to Fields. Fields thought it an excellent idea and, subject to approval by Dali, proposed the delay be put into action immediately. Dali agreed. So did Fields.

Officials, however, insisted that the players should be ready to commence in five minutes.

And so it was that at 4:38 p.m. Dali and Fields found themselves being ushered back to Court 3, Dali claiming he had now been waiting for so long he was beginning to see things and Fields claiming to have been bitten on the fibula by a Tibetan mountain yak during an attempt to get a hat down from a tree. When informed there were no yaks in France he said he was pleased to hear it and maybe now they'd stop biting people. Dali then described some of the things he had seen and the umpire ordered both players to be tested for stimulants. The match itself was conducted in good heart, Fields producing some delightful play, particularly his footwork, and it was no surprise to see Chaplin in the crowd, enjoying himself immensely.

At two sets up and 4–2 in the fourth Fields chased an angled crosscourt smash from Dali, got to it and threw up a very high lob. Dali ran back and waited for it, let it bounce and smashed it again, this time deep into the other corner. Fields never reappeared.

The drug tests established that Fields had been playing with a blood alcohol level of 24 percent but that Dali showed no trace of any illegal substance. "That's a relief," said Fields by phone, "although poor old Dali's obviously got a few problems."

In the women's draw events were slightly less alarming, Maria Montessori going through against Constance Markievicz (one of the Gore-Booth sisters who did so well here as juniors), Virginia Stephen-Woolf (one of the Stephen sisters who did so well here as juniors) eventually getting on top of Katherine Mansfield (one of the Beauchamp sisters who did so well here as juniors) and Anna Pavlova impressive against Melanie Klein.

As dusk began to close around the arena and the lights came up, the controversial Magritte emerged onto Centre Court with his opponent, the marvelous Greek Nikos Kazantzakis. Magritte has been in fabulous form and tonight was magical. He mixed his game up beautifully and Kazantzakis had trouble picking what was coming. Magritte would appear to be setting up for a forehand and would hit a backhand. He would move into position to hit a smash and instead would let the ball bounce and hit a different shot altogether. Only the Greek's great passion kept him in the match. His compatriots appear at this tournament with (Hel) after their name. Kazantzakis alone insists on (Gre). He took the third set and did a lap of honor in tunic and sandals, punching the air. Normal transmission was soon resumed, however, and the talented Belgian came away with the win.

Day 18

Bernhardt v. Lenya • Barnes v. Chanel • Picasso v. Beckett • MacNeice v. Levi • Krishnamurti v. Russell • Prokofiev v. Tolstoy • Freud v. Casals

The sensation of the day occurred in the afternoon. Sarah Bernhardt and Coco Chanel had been cheered from the arena after good wins, the heroic Bernhardt draped in the French flag, Chanel in a little black dress.

The illuminated sign at the end of the Centre Court now read PICASSO V. BECKETT. The match was delayed while a group of oil and movie people were photographed on court with Picasso in an atmosphere made up of equal parts radical chic and celebrity bullfight.

The Beckett people were also there but were quiet and slightly bored. They didn't care where they sat, they purchased no memorabilia and some of them watched the entire match without dismounting from bicycles. Beckett, who has represented his country in both tennis and cricket, is very handy in a tough spot, which is exactly where he quickly found himself today.

Picasso came out firing on all six and for a while appeared to do no wrong. He is strong and his footwork is excellent. Beckett kept the ball in play a lot and, like Satie, encouraged the expectation that he would vary the play, and then didn't. Picasso slipped away again in the second to win it 6–4. In the third set, however, he played to the crowd and began to spray his returns. As the replay showed, Beckett's approach in the fourth was very simple. He hit the ball to Picasso's strengths, his big forehand and that wonderful sliced backhand. Picasso found himself hitting six or eight superb shots in one rally but getting six or eight returns coming back at him like familiar friends. As the match wore on Beckett began to hit the ball later and very high and the player most famous for his speed would rush into position and wait. As the pauses got longer, people began to laugh. Someone asked a woman near the press box, "What are you laughing at?"

"Nothing," she smiled.

The fifth set consisted of Picasso hitting the ball even harder, thereby lengthening the pauses generated by Beckett. He achieved everything except a victory and Beckett won the match by successfully resisting defeat.

There will also be drinks from the upper shelf in Ireland and doubles at the BBC tonight following the performance of Louis MacNeice, who has never gotten past the first round of a tournament before. "Normally I'm playing against Auden," he said. Today he played classic tennis to see off the Italian Carlo Levi.

"I'm on some sort of medication," said MacNeice. "So how I got up today I don't quite know."

Levi was philosophical. "Louis is underrated," he said. "Normally he's playing against Auden."

It is not clear what MacNeice is on medication for. "They won't tell me," he said. He is undergoing tests and so far only problems associated with potholing and liver dysfunction have been ruled out. "If I knew what the problem was," said the silken Ulsterman, "I wouldn't be on medication and I wouldn't be in the same half of the draw as Auden."

There were some difficulties late in the day during the match between the elegant Indian Jiddu Krishnamurti and the pigeon-chested Englishman Little Bertie Russell. Krishnamurti doesn't hold with concepts such as "left," "right," "in," "out" or "fault." He also refuses to concede that the aim of the game is "to win." Russell believes the game's administration must be "transparent and democratic." Both players agreed that balls would not be called "in" or "out" or "fault" but "good shot," "bad luck" and "sorry." They agreed that the umpire for their match must come from a dissident faction in an African nation not dependent on international capital.

As a consequence their match began ten minutes late with a great deal of mutual goodwill and a Nova Scotian in the chair. There was some suggestion that Nova Scotia is not in Africa although this was dismissed by Krishnamurti who does not accept the term "in." The Indian played "good shot" tennis in the first set, strayed into an amount of "bad luck" in the second and lost some precision in his serving for rather a lot of "sorry" in the third. The match was therefore "won" by Russell, who is traveling nicely and now goes on to meet the Spockster in what even the mystical Indian is prepared to concede might be the next round.

Tonight's Centre Court match was again fraught with an increasingly familiar tension. Russian authorities want victories but feel threatened by the players who achieve them.

Ukrainian Sergei Prokofiev was national junior champion at the astonishing age of eight. He looks tentative and watchful.

"It is true," he said. "I am a tentative and watchful person."

Is he worried about anything?

"Nothing in particular."

Has he been happy playing here?

"I love playing anywhere, yes."

Is it true that, while he was playing, his room was searched?

"I'm not sure about that. I might have left the shutters open. It is possible a breeze entered the room from below and blew all my stuff out the window and up five floors and in through the window of the suite where the Russian Tennis Federation are staying."

At the other end tonight was the man known on the circuit as the Count, the oldest player in the tournament. Leo Tolstoy was Russian Army champion as a young man, won the French two years before his opponent today was born and went on to rewrite the record books. He twice won the Grand Slam, both times taking men's and mixed doubles titles at all four majors (with Warren Pearce and the late Anna Karenina). He fought for better conditions for players and spectators, was instrumental in the development of youth programs and, in a move which ultimately brought about the breakup of his marriage, recently announced that he would no longer be receiving appearance fees, tournament winnings or other income from any source. The Centre Court crowd included dignitaries from all over the world, including Mahatma Gandhi and the French president. Tolstoy is adored here in France even though he has never lost to a French player and regards the French, as a nation, as "vermin."

Sergei Prokofiev wasn't just playing the Count, he was playing the history of the sport. He lost the first two sets but took the third 6–2 with some of the most commanding tennis we've seen all week and big old Leo must have wondered how many Prokofievs there were. In the fourth set Tolstoy opened the throttle in the eleventh game to break Prokofiev and then served out the match 7–5. An hour later Prokofiev was called to a crisis meeting with the Russian authorities and was dropped from the Davis Cup squad.

The day finished with thirteenth-seeded Austrian handful

Nabokov has had more written about him than most players competing at this event. Photographs of him with a butterfly net have been beamed around the world with descriptions of his play as "taut, important and sublime." None of these things have ever been said about Ring Lardner, who was photographed after the match holding a tennis racquet.

Franz Kafka got a very big fright tonight and, if anyone wishes to witness an unusual spectacle, Franz Kafka getting a very big fright would be among the more rewarding of those currently available. He came out against Damon Runyon and found himself in all sorts of trouble. On his day Runyon is capable of knocking over the tall timber. His court speed is terrific and his volleying deadly. After the first set, Kafka must have wondered whether Runyon was ever going to leave him alone. In the second set Kafka hustled, he chased everything and he rushed the net whenever he could.

Untroubled by these events, Runyon has a good look at everything Kafka sends over and then hauls off and hits it very hard with old Mr. Racquet.

At 2–5, Kafka sat in his chair, drenched in perspiration, his legs exhausted and his mind racing. Runyon's friends gave every indication of having engaged in short-term investments bearing on the result and with their man two sets up and 3–0 in the third set they were helping themselves to plenty of goulash and some "special" coffee provided by a citizen named Toots. Kafka was up against it in spades.

He steadied, broke Runyon with some superb returns to get to 2–3, served four aces and broke Runyon again to get it to 4–3, held serve and broke Runyon again for the set.

In the fourth Kafka was untouchable. His final shot was a ball picked up from deep in the back corner and whipped down the line. Runyon simply smiled and walked to the net. He said later he thought Kafka would become "a very prominent player indeed," that he had enjoyed himself more than somewhat and had done "nicely," even picking up a little scratch on a business proposition involving the 3:20 at Longchamp.

Day 20

Millay v. Rand • Escher v. Schweitzer • Einstein v. Thurber • Conrad v. Faulkner • Jung v. Hesse • Shaw v. Keaton • Ford v. Orwell

Officials were confronted with a protest tonight over the result of the Edna St. Vincent Millay v. Ayn Rand match, won by Millay. In a detailed submission Rand claimed "these points (see schedule 2) were scored incorrectly within the meaning of the Rules. They should be replayed, witnessed and scored accurately and I will win them."

"It is unthinkable I should be knocked out," Rand told reporters. "I am clearly the best player and I will fucking win. Simple as that."

If anyone has a lazy hundred, a small bet on a Davis Cup

victory sometime soon for Holland might be worth a thought. The bookies don't think they can do it but cut this out and stick it on the fridge. They've got four players in this tournament: Mondrian, who went out in the first round to Casals but was playing with two broken ribs, de Kooning, van Gogh and Maurits Escher, who was in devastating form against the German Bert Schweitzer today.

Schweitzer is no slouch and he didn't do much wrong but at one stage he served to Escher's backhand and Escher hit a beautiful forehand winner for 0–15. Schweitzer's next serve was to Escher's forehand. Escher hit a backhand winner for 0–30. Schweitzer served again, curving into the body. Escher somehow fended it back and Schweitzer hit a crosscourt drive into the ad court and was passed by a shot coming back from the deuce court. He did his best to understand but it was beyond him and the crowd went very quiet. A few people cleared their throats and there was some fiddling with programs. "I didn't know where I was," said Schweitzer. "He was playing angles that weren't there."

Also big with the angles was Albert Einstein, the electromagnetic wizard with the high-pitched laugh. His approach was almost casual against big Jim Thurber today. He turned up late because of what he described as "some sort of mix-up with the time." As a result the match began twenty-five minutes after it officially ended, although Einstein said they could finish on time if they got on with it. He quickly got himself out to 6–0 and 4–0. Half an hour later he found himself at 6–0, 4–6, 0–6 to an opponent who was checking line calls, not because he questioned them, but because he couldn't see the ball. Einstein stepped up the pace and took the fourth set but Thurber, who said later he had a number of dogs watching the event on television, peeled off a series of unplayable returns to go out to 5–2 in the fifth. Einstein pegged him back but he is a very lucky boy and seems to be vulnerable to an attack which is purely defensive. "Jim," said Thurber's wife Helen, "I think we've all done very well. It's time to go home."

Sixth-seed Joseph Conrad was this afternoon trying to work out what had gone wrong against the doughty Bill Faulkner. Conrad stuck to his game plan but he lacked imagination and, when his game plan wasn't working, he stuck to his game plan.

"I didn't feel sharp at any stage out there today," said Conrad. "Faulkner is very good and I couldn't seem to get anything going. I don't know anymore. You come to these tournaments. There are players you've never heard of. There are women. It used to be an honest struggle for muscular Christians. Now it's just chaos."

There have been questions about Faulkner's fitness and he often struggles to find form early in a tournament. "Everybody struggles," he says. "There would be no point to any of this if it weren't a struggle. Joe said it used to be a struggle for muscular Christians. I think it's a damn struggle for everyone. But I believe we will prevail."

Carl Jung very nearly followed Conrad out, having to pull

out all the stops against Hermann Hesse. Both players are cult figures on the American circuit and a full house of younger fans watched wide-eyed as the Jungmeister eventually got on top of the Hermanator.

If George Shaw is to be believed, his opponent today, the undemonstrative American Buster Keaton, is "one of the most remarkable players in the world." Shaw spoke to the press before their match because he had "another engagement" afterwards. He said he thought he would win because Keaton's opponent would be harder for Keaton to deal with than Shaw's would be for Shaw. He said he intended to control the match from the back of the court but to come in on Keaton's backhand and to keep the ball low at all times.

"Keaton is completely unfazed by anything overhead and is at his best when he seems most exposed," he said. "If his position looks hopeless he'll run away with the match and my only hope is to beat him in a contest he thinks he can win. I'll need to concentrate."

It's hard to know which was more impressive, Shaw's play or the remarks he made about his intentions before he started. He was right about Keaton, right about the match and right about himself.

Ford Madox Ford, onetime hoofer and a longtime regular on the European tour, might have hoped for an easier second-round assignment than George Orwell, the player many regard as the pick of the English crop at this tournament. From similar backgrounds, both players began their careers outside England. Ford kicked off in France and Orwell in Burma and Spain where he got to the quarters in the Spanish Open and pulled out when he discovered that many of the Spanish amateurs were actually German and Russian professionals. Opposed to the administration of the game in Germany and disenchanted with its management in Russia, he was critical of the international governing bodies and the role of the media. There are many tournaments to which Orwell is not invited, and others which he refuses to enter.

Plenty made the trip out to Court 6 this morning just to see what he looked like. Be it known, he looked very good. He will be the subject of detailed study across the channel tonight at Ladbrokes and in other academies of likelihood.

Round
3

Day 21

Mann v. Satie • de Beauvoir v. Draper • Malraux v. MacNeice • Derain v. Yeats • Einstein v. Steinbeck • Keynes v. Kafka

The third-round singles matches began today in a schedule which was to include men's and women's doubles and mixed-doubles matches but players turned up this morning to find that everything had changed.

"All doubles matches have been postponed," read the announcement, "and will commence to coincide with the fourth round."

This is a mark of respect to the German player Karl Liebnecht, whose body was found this morning in a lane not far from the main concourse. He had been shot in the back of the head. Here to play in the mixed with Rosa Luxemburg, Liebnecht was active in his opposition to German tennis administration.

Luxemburg faced the press this morning, looking drawn but determined. "Karl was murdered by his own countrymen," she said. "The police will find he was killed by German bullets, because he fought against the domination and manipulation of German tennis by one group. This is not happening only in our country. Many other brave people will also soon be killed by the administration in their own countries. We could still stop this but we won't. The press won't let us. Watch how many newspapers print this story."

Luxemburg was wrong about that. Most of the press carried the story and it received wide coverage on television. There were two major versions of what had happened. One was headlined PARANOID POLISH WHORE ACCUSES GERMAN AUTHORITIES OF MURDERING WORTHLESS SHIT and the other was DANGEROUS CRIMINAL SHOT TRYING TO ESCAPE.

Of the massive German contingent which arrived in Paris, only Mann and Einstein remain in the draw and both are openly critical of current German tennis officialdom. Nike president Friedrich Nietzsche has initiated legal proceedings against German organizers for attributing to him remarks expressing the idea that German players were supermen. "What I said in fact," he claimed, "was exactly the opposite."

At 10 a.m. Thomas Mann called a press conference and attempted to say something but the sound system went dead, a hot dog stand blew up and the press tent caught fire. Matches were delayed for two hours while power was restored and officers checked the concourse for suspicious persons or other "devices."

When the tennis started there was a concerted attempt to pretend that nothing had happened. It was obvious to everyone at the stadium, however, that the atmosphere was full of menace.

Thomas Mann's previous matches were on outside courts but he was in the lion's den this morning against the subtlety and placement of Eric Satie, who worked out what Mann was doing and began to steam his mail open. Every time Mann tried something different, Satie was on to it. Mann stopped booming his serve in and concentrated on accuracy; Satie boomed his returns in, crowded the net and forced the error. When Mann got the trainer out to look at a problem with one of his feet, Satie got his uncle out to look at some photographs. Satie and coach Jim Nopidies had worked on their rhythm and it was nearly the German's undoing.

"Satie is a tricky opponent," said Mann later, "because it's hard to know what he's going to do until he works out what you're trying to do."

Satie said Mann played "superbly" and predicts big things for him "if he can get past Magritte."

The French turned out in droves for the next match between the empress Simone de Beauvoir and little-known American Ruth Draper. A sensation was quickly on the cards here as de Beauvoir, playing as if the result were a formality, was put on notice that every point would be contested and that Draper had studied her game in detail. Draper was quick and efficient and the crowd watched in quiet dismay as she punched hole after hole in one of the great defenses in modern tennis. The American was on the wrong end of some very dubious line calls to lose the second but she then raced out to 3–0 in the final set before the dame set off after her. Draper then became distracted by a small wooden aircraft flying low overhead. This was enough for de Beauvoir to clamber back in for a win. But she did not look like a champion today and she certainly didn't feel like one.

"Simone is a great player," said Draper. "And she's not easy to play. One thing about German tennis, incidentally, is the influence it's having on Italian tennis. If they go the same way I fear for many of my friends."

In a statement released tonight it was revealed that Draper's friend Lauro de Bossis, an Italian opposed to the current administration of German tennis and to its influence on Italian tennis, had this afternoon appeared over Rome in a wooden plane, throwing out leaflets encouraging Italian players "not to allow the game in Italy to be run by Germany." His plane has not been found. Ms. Draper is said to be "inconsolable."

The crowd knew nothing of this, and was then presented with the more edifying sight of André Malraux carrying French hopes against Louis MacNeice. Auden, who was there to watch his friend MacNeice, said after the match that both players had performed brilliantly. He added that "the German tennis authorities have started rounding up Jews and dissident players in Germany. The head of the German Tennis Academy set the press tent on fire while Mann was talking. Mann and his family cannot return to Germany and are not permitted to leave France. I would like to announce that his daughter Erika and I were married half an hour ago and that as a result she will be able to remain in England, whither she has now departed."

The next unit in the French line on Centre Court was the self-styled Parisian "wild beast" André Derain. He was up against Big Bill Yeats, who sometimes plays as if he's in a dream and sometimes as if he's starring in a movie about his own life. Today he settled into his work well before spotting Maud Gonne and her daughter Iseult high up in the northern stand, at which point he lost four games, broke his racquet and came out in a prickly rash. Covered in creams and soothing unguents he then lost the next three games and sat in the mist, moaning like a wounded stag. Gonne quietly made her way down from her eyrie and left.

Yeats regrouped and won two games before noticing Iseult trying to scramble down behind the stand onto the back of a truck. He lost the next five games and scratched the skin off part of his face. As the fifth set began his brother Jack, a great friend of Beckett and a handy player himself, encouraged him to get a grip.

Big Bill went to the back of the court, did a number of deep knee bends and stood with his eyes closed for some time. He then served with greater power, moved like a panther and his fortunes changed. Changed utterly. Derain tried everything, but

Yeats had his mind back on the job and was in full sail.

In an interesting afternoon, Plum Wodehouse, who appears tomorrow with partner Chris Isherwood as one half of the celebrated "Woodies" doubles team, took on the resourceful Herbie Wells in the singles. Plum ran everything down and by the third set he was chairman of the board, putting his passing shots exactly where he wanted them. He was thrilled that George and Ira Gershwin, and the injured Cole Porter, were present at the match.

Wodehouse was in hot water later over comments he made during an interview with German radio. Asked what he thought of the state of German tennis he said, "Yes, very good. Can't see what all the fuss is about. I'm a great admirer of German tennis and of your Teuton generally."

Albert Einstein made short work of his match with John Steinbeck this afternoon, clearing the decks with his service game and cleaning up where necessary from the net. Steinbeck likes to have a real swing at the ball and several times he saw the return pass him before he completed his shot. "This guy's the business," he said. "There wasn't much I could do today."

The Russian Anna Akhmatova might have wilted in the heat against Josephine Baker but was resolute and said afterwards, "I am opposed to everything that is going on in Russia at the moment except its Russianness."

Keynes' fitness was always going to be a concern in his tussle with Kafka. A demanding five-setter in the first round and a huge second-round win over Paderewski had taken a heavy toll, especially for a man with a history of shinsplints. These were problems compounded by the angular Czech, who even ran to where balls would have landed if they hadn't gone into the net.

"There is no need to get to those," called Keynes.

"How do we know that?" said Kafka. He won the first two sets to love and as the players changed ends Keynes proposed that, since he hadn't won a game and his position was "frankly hopeless," the tournament "lend" him a set, to get him going. Kafka had no objection and the scoreboard was altered to read: F. Kafka (Czech) two sets, J. M. Keynes (Eng) one set.

This changed the Englishman's approach. With a set up his sleeve he had a real go at his first serve and Kafka stood so far back to receive he became distracted by the attention of a young woman sitting in front of him and seemed to lose concentration. Keynes won 6–4 and set sail in the fifth (fourth) before Kafka, sensing a disaster, began to regain his composure. From this point Kafka didn't do much wrong and, although Keynes' revolutionary suggestion helped make a match of it, the little Czech won it in five (four). The full score was F. Kafka d. J. M. Keynes 6–0, 6–0, (6–7*), 4–6, 6–4.

* Set advanced to Keynes and carried as a debit against the fourth, which becomes 2–1 to Kafka with an interest related debt of one (1) set secured over Keynes' holdings in the fifth. Kafka wins four sets to minus one.
Signed:
Witnessed:
Dated:

Day 22

Chekhov v. Muir • Magritte v. Hecht • Beckett v. Munch • Russell v. Spock • Proust v. Puccini • Bierce v. van Gogh • Dali v. Jung

Tony Chekhov cruised into the fourth round today, though his opponent, the Orkney-born qualifier Edwin Muir, put together "the best set and a half of tennis I think I've ever played." When Muir took the second set to a tie-break Chekhov applauded him and then simply got on with the job. He said afterwards that he could not comment on his play. "I was not in the audience. I did not see my play. I have reports that it went well. That is good. I must go to Moscow."

René Magritte had all the answers against the American Ben Hecht in a virtually error-free exhibition. In the second set, in particular, he played complete games facing the other way, hitting the ball back through his legs while looking at Hecht's image reflected in the sunglasses of a service lineswoman. It was a visual treat and a hint of what was to come.

Samuel Beckett prefers playing on an outside court and took some time adjusting to the main arena this morning. There were other complications beforehand, said friends. His mother was present and he required some treatment for boils, Peggy Guggenheim was present, his wife Suzanne was present, Joyce's daughter was present, someone called the Smeraldina was present and a very nice woman from the BBC was present.

He toyed with the idea of not going on. "I can't go on," he said. But, realizing Eddie Munch's problems were worse than his own, he changed his mind. "I'll go on," he said.

The self-absorbed Munch, who couldn't even get a wild card into the Norwegian Open, exhausted by two tough matches and a skein of family bereavements, makes Beckett look like Bing Crosby. During the warm-up Munch could barely hold his head up and when play started he dragged himself to the baseline and waited like a condemned man.

If the first set had any bright moments the crowd couldn't find them. Munch, paler than ever, played with little interest and Beckett spent the set looking at the ground in case he caught sight of anyone. Neither player deserved to win it and neither did, although after a very long time Munch did at least lose it. It was the only set he did lose.

Beckett predicted that the Norwegian would go well. "He won't win the tournament, doesn't want to win it and doesn't care who does. And yet he is here, playing his best, knowing things can only get worse."

Little Bertie Russell was looking good against the Spockster until his family turned up. One of the Russell children made a noise during a rally and at the conclusion of the point Little Bertie walked over to the players' box, where they were sitting, and yelled, "Will you be quiet! Can't you see I'm playing?" At 4–0 in the second set one of the ballgirls fell over near the baseline and Russell rushed over and fell on top of her. Momentarily distracted by a muffled sobbing from one of his children, he stood up and smashed his racquet into the ground. "I'm not going to mention this again!" he shouted at the child. "Shut the fuck up while Daddy's working!"

Spock approached Russell. "I don't think you should be talking to a child like that. You, of all people, must know how important early childhood is."

Russell bristled. "Oh," he said. "Doesn't that rather depend on what we mean by 'know'?"

When this happened Russell was 6–0 and 4–0. He didn't win another game. Spock was magnificent.

Highly fancied indigenous phoenix Marcel Proust was back to his best today against the lyrical Puccini. What a comeback this was from the translucent Proust, a touch player whose accuracy has earned him the appellation "M. le Drop," but whose health seems to operate along the lines of a raffle. Everything Puccini does, by contrast, is structured. He often plays three closely contested sets with the brightest sections reserved for the closing moments and the tie-breaks. Against a resurgent Proust he became frustrated and lost concentration. Had he been more adaptable he might have seized the third set but Proust did what a lot of players won't do when they hit trouble. He took his medicine, learned his lesson and moved on.

Ambrose Bierce was leading Vincent van Gogh with a set in hand when van Gogh came out and served a game made up completely of double faults, destroying much of the net and removing a section of paneling in the back wall. The laser unit which measures service speed emitted a high-pitched wail, displayed the legend 722 kmh and has not operated since. Van Gogh was in despair.

Bierce needed only to stay out of trouble to go through. Staying out of trouble, however, is not Ambrose Bierce's long suit and he proposed to the umpire that van Gogh be allowed to serve with no line calls. "If the ball is a fault or a shot is out, don't call it, just keep a record of it. Leave him alone." Bierce then sat down and refused to play "until you let him play without yelling at him." No great advocate of the system, Bierce did not attend the opening ceremony, the official American team dinner, the press club luncheon or the sponsors' banquet. When asked if he had deliberately avoided these functions he said he had no idea they were on. He was disappointed not to have been told, he said, particularly in the case of the sponsors' banquet, which he would very much have enjoyed deliberately avoiding.

When play resumed, no line calls were made. Freed of the conventions of scoring, van Gogh moved faster, hit the ball with greater topspin and made much better use of the court. He played shots no one else would have attempted in what was a memorable display. Tennis authorities, who an hour and a half earlier had regarded him as a rogue bull, were all over him like cousins as he stood in the bright yellow light signing autographs. Bierce spoke to him briefly, shook him warmly by the hand and left the arena. He hasn't been seen since. Friends think he may be in Bolivia.

Two players more different in style and attitude than Salvador Dali and Carl Jung would be hard to imagine. Jung is often called upon by other players to help with a footwork problem, a crisis of confidence or a faulty service action. In Sam Beckett's case, for example, Jung opened up his stance and allowed Beckett to "play properly." He is even capable of analyzing himself, or "myselves" as he calls them: the Jung with the talent and the Jung with the brains. He was listed to play doubles with Freud but following a boat trip during which the Doc accused Jung of resenting him because he was his father, Jung discreetly rearranged his schedule and is now playing doubles by himself.

Dali, who appeared at the launch on a silver tray with an apple in his mouth, says he isn't trying to work anything out at all and has never approached Jung for advice. As he says, "This artist was never a Jung man."

It was always going to be an absorbing contest and by midway through the second set commentators were sending out for new ways of describing what they were looking at. Jung, a great reader of other players, quickly reaches an understanding of what he's up against. In Dali's case he worked out that he was in a confined space with a player who sought a great deal of attention and was beating the pants off him. Dali didn't work anything out, he just played spectacular tennis although there was debate as to whether the term "hat" adequately covers what Dali had on his head. At some stages Dali himself was barely visible. There was just a "swish" and the ball came flying over the net toward the various Jungs.

Dali was spoken to by authorities following the press conference which he attended dressed as Louis XIV. "Stand well back," he shouted. "I need room to masturbate."

Day 23

Seurat v. Waller • Lardner v. Chaplin • Wittgenstein v. Hasek • Shaw v. Eliot • Stein v. McCarthy • Tolstoy v. Mayakovsky

Georges Seurat's challenge came unstuck today against Fats Waller, whose warm-up is desultory and who was using a borrowed racquet because he had forgotten his own. "Staying at home," he muttered. "Too tired." The minute he starts playing, however, there is nothing else going on. Seurat is an experienced campaigner and is aware of the significance of every point but, even when he pulled Waller back in the second set, Waller took it in a tie-break and ran away again in the third like a kid at a Christmas party.

"Charlie's Army" was out in force today; they wear bowler

hats and slightly oversized shoes and many of them twirl little canes when things are going well. There was a good deal of cane-twirling today until Ring Lardner decided on a different tack. At the beginning of the second set he decided Lardner wasn't going to play Chaplin; he was going to make Chaplin play Lardner.

Lardner took the first game and then in the second he stood right up to the Chaplin service, hit it on the up and got in to the net. He lost the first three points but Chaplin put a forehand wide and was not happy. He then put two returns into the net and was very annoyed. He lost the game and threw his racquet on the ground. Lardner called "Sorry" and the crowd laughed.

Lardner held for 3–0 and broke again, this time by hitting the ball very late past Chaplin as he came in.

The little tramp was furious. He lost his serve again at 4–4 in the third set, Lardner took it 6–4 and was 3–0 in the fourth before Chaplin got back on the board. By now the crowd knew they were watching something very unusual; a player who can take apart an opponent before the opponent realizes it. Very little has been written about Ring Lardner, except by Henry Mencken, who has been practicing with him, and by Damon Runyon, who revealed: "I have plenty of 80–1 on Mr. Lardner before the matter commences as I believe him to be very handy indeed." But it was Mencken whose headline, above his syndicated column, best captured it: CHAPLIN STEPS INTO RING. RING STEPS INTO CHAPLIN.

It is difficult to know whether Ludwig Wittgenstein plays

tennis because he enjoys it or because it keeps him from doing something he would enjoy. He is not the most relaxed character in town; he looks tense and anxious ("haunted" according to the newspapers) and friends say he needs to be "tricked" into going to sleep or practicing. "No," he says, "I do not play well enough to practice."

Although he and his opponent today, the Czech Jaroslav Hasek, are six years apart and from different countries, both came up through the Austrian army, an experience Hasek describes as "hilarious" and Wittgenstein as "appalling."

Hasek has performed high deeds here so far; he took out the all-surface specialist Wally Gropius in the first round and out-finished Jean Sibelius in the second. Wittgenstein began slowly against the American Williams and then took Lawrence of Nottingham apart in the second round. (The sight of the perspiring Lawrence sitting proud and shirtless between sets steaming like a horse and Wittgenstein staring in unblinking fury at his racquet belied the facts of the match.)

Not everyone is impressed with Wittgenstein. Karl Popper, who missed Austrian selection because of a coaching appointment in New Zealand but who is here to practice with Einstein, says, "In order to establish that someone is a great player we should not look for evidence that he is, we should look for evidence that he is not. If we cannot find it, we might conclude he is a great player." And in Wittgenstein's case? "Why do you think he won't come out to the practice courts?"

Hasek can consider himself unlucky to have lost this match. He lost the first set with an ace which was called out (which both players protested about and which the replay showed quite clearly was in) and the second on a foot fault called from the other end. His ground strokes in the third set were unplayable but at 3–3 in the final set he fell heavily on his left knee, lost something of his speed and that was that.

Take nothing away from Wittgenstein in this. He was never out of it and said afterwards he was learning to put the ball "just out of reach." Earlier on, he said, he had been trying to put the ball "out of reach." Now he realizes he needs only to put it "just out of reach."

There was no love lost on Court 4 last night with an Irishman and an American up against each other in what was a very English battle. Both players have done much for English tennis, Shaw enlivening its structures and forcing it to understand its own politics and Eliot finding an expression for its despair and loss of meaning. For two sets Shaw looked like an admiral, timing the ball well and serving superbly. As the match progressed, however, Eliot played the big points better, although he was annoyed when Shaw suggested that he attend to his wife who had just fainted for the fifth time. Eliot said later his wife was "perfectly well but was overcome by heat."

"Eliot is a good player," said Shaw, "a poor judge, a bad husband and a racist."

This perhaps relates to the statement Eliot released earlier:

"The tragic death of Karl Liebnecht, a Jew who was opposed to the usurpation of power and sponsorship money in the hands of one class, throws into question the claim often made by Jews that they do not wish to control the sponsorship money."

There wasn't much doubt that Gertrude Stein would say something about this following her match with Mary McCarthy. Or that McCarthy would agree with her. What was surprising was that Rosa Luxemburg, who was visibly upset throughout her match with the Indian Sarojini Naidu, would be arrested at the post-match press conference and taken away for questioning.

"Questioning by whom?" asked Naidu. "Where is she?"

"Questioning by the authorities," she was told. "A routine matter."

Vita Sackville-West was loose in her match and Frances Hodgkins goes through to meet Bernhardt in the fourth round. Sackville-West is unusual in that she was put down for this tournament at birth although due to a filing error she discovered she had been entered in the men's draw and was, in fact, a woman.

The departure of Eleanor Roosevelt, of whom the same might be said, was also a surprise although she has invested a good deal of her energy into securing the right to multiple partners in the doubles. Maxine Elliott, who beat Roosevelt today, is a gifted player whose partner Anthony Wilding has won three successive Wimbledon singles crowns.

Tonight's match featured the Count, who sent down a few

range-finders against his countryman Vladimir Mayakovsky and then opened the throttle with a towering service game. There's something about Mayakovsky when he's got his back to the wall, however, and he summoned his reserves today, stood his ground and fought his way to a remarkable victory. In a match that went out live and was seen by an astonishing 27 percent of the population of western Europe, Mayakovsky ran the legs off the older man, got to the net and dictated terms. In the final set he stood back and beat him at his own game. The Count knew it was all over and afterwards observed, "All victories are the same but every defeat is a defeat in its own way."

Mayakovsky put it for many: "Without Leo Tolstoy the game in Russia would still be played with sticks and dried manure. More than any other player of his era, he is one of us."

Round 4

Day 24

Malraux v. Einstein • Bernhardt v. Hodgkins • Nijinsky and Pavlova v. Benchley and Parker • Kafka v. Wittgenstein

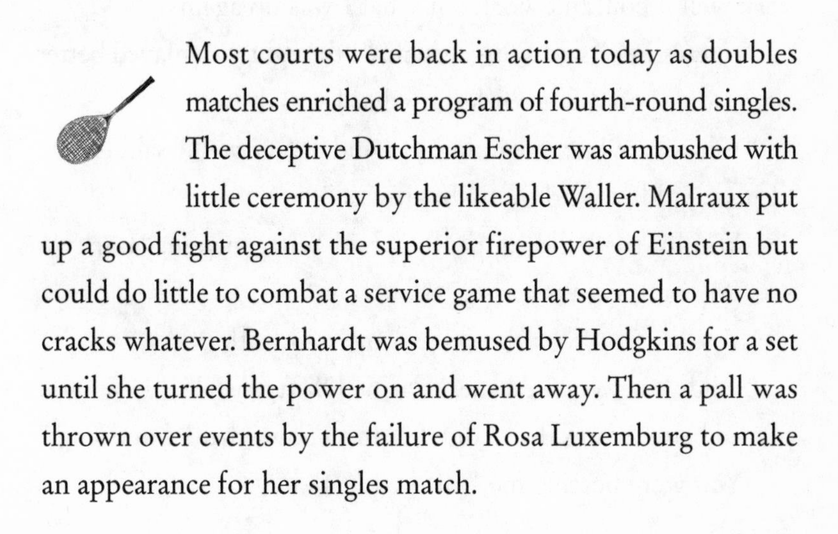

Most courts were back in action today as doubles matches enriched a program of fourth-round singles. The deceptive Dutchman Escher was ambushed with little ceremony by the likeable Waller. Malraux put up a good fight against the superior firepower of Einstein but could do little to combat a service game that seemed to have no cracks whatever. Bernhardt was bemused by Hodgkins for a set until she turned the power on and went away. Then a pall was thrown over events by the failure of Rosa Luxemburg to make an appearance for her singles match.

On outside courts, seeded doubles combination Brecht and Weill were outclassed by Shostakovich and Prokofiev, and Hope and Crosby played entertaining tennis in taking out Bakst and the Russian Blok, formerly the Soviet Blok. In the women's doubles the Americans Roosevelt and Luce were beaten by Lotte Lenya and Marlene Dietrich. Second-seeded mixed doubles combination Nijinsky and Pavlova looked great but they only just beat Benchley and Dorothy Parker, whose approach might be described as "social." Aside from his own service Nijinsky did not hit a ball and it was left to Pavlova to sprint about the place spinning and twirling, leaping and diving. She finished the match completely exhausted, surrounded by flowers thrown from the stands, while Nijinsky stood at the net, glaring at a cloud.

Kafka said after their match that Wittgenstein had "played very well. I couldn't work out what I was up against."

"Interesting," said Wittgenstein. "I thought you played better than I did. I couldn't work out what I was doing."

"Whatever you were doing, you did it very well," said Kafka. "I just couldn't work out what it was."

"You hit the ball beautifully," said Wittgenstein. "For two sets you sat me on my arse."

"Yes, but you won three sets," insisted Kafka.

"I didn't say you beat me," clarified Wittgenstein. "I said you played better tennis than I did. I didn't know what I was doing."

"You were beating me," offered Kafka.

"That was a *consequence* of what I was doing," corrected Wittgenstein.

"It must have been, in part, a consequence of what *I* was doing," parried Kafka.

"I thought you said you didn't know what you were up against."

Kafka looked confused and said rather elliptically that he was glad nothing had fallen on him.

The news about Rosa Luxemburg was contained in an official communiqué. "The troubled Polish star," it began, "finds that due to other commitments she must withdraw from the tournament."

Reaction was immediate. "It is not the truth," said George Orwell, preparing for his match against Munch tomorrow. "Look at the language of the communiqué. It hides the truth. It is necessary to make the statement only because it is not true. Where is Rosa Luxemburg?"

A large deputation of women players registered a formal protest. Sarojini Naidu, beaten by Luxemburg in the previous round and half of the Naidu–Pandit team that took out the fashionable Schiaparelli–Chanel combination today, was distraught. "This is a lie full of lies. Rosa is not troubled, is not a star, has no other commitments and has not withdrawn from the tournament. Rosa's friend Karl Liebnecht has been murdered, and now she has been abducted herself. Rosa is being persecuted and possibly tortured because of her thinking about the game. This is a defining moment. Rosa Luxemburg must be brought back here immediately and allowed to play. Moreover, she and every other participant must be given a guarantee of safety by the tournament itself."

Tournament officials are tonight "considering the position."

Day 25

Stravinsky v. Rodo • Munch v. Orwell • Proust v. Dali • Arendt v. Mandelstam • Chekhov and Miller v. Lardner and Fitzgerald • Riefenstahl and Hari v. Mead and Stark

Igor Stravinsky slipped past Diego Rivera in the first round and played a Homeric five-setter against Pasternak before a tough exam against Sean O'Casey in the third round.

His opponent today, Uruguayan qualifier José Rodo, has lifted the profile of South American tennis and was not disgraced today by any means but there is an experimental quality to everything Stravinsky does and it's not always obvious what he is about. Today he seemed scrappy and loose but there was never any doubt about the score.

"Look at the score," he said afterwards. "Read it. It's all there."

"Were you nervous?" asked Norman Mailer.

"Nervous?"

"Yes," Mailer continued. "You seemed anxious."

"Anxious?" he asked. "How?"

"Your playing seems anxious."

"My playing seems anxious?" repeated Stravinsky. "In what way?"

"Your playing makes the crowd anxious. It is not soothing. It is not calming."

Stravinsky held up his hand. "The crowd should be soothed?"

"Perhaps if the crowd is anxious," Mailer explained, "it should be soothed."

Stravinsky was still not clear. "Are you saying the crowd is anxious or are you asking me if I am anxious?"

"I am saying there is anxiety in the way you play."

"I see," said Stravinsky. "But why do you say that?"

"I say that because the way you play makes me anxious."

"You are anxious," said Stravinsky. "Of course you are. I'm not surprised. Where is Rosa Luxemburg?"

The wheels finally came off the Eddie Munch wagon this afternoon but the Norwegian leaves a lasting impression. He was completely exhausted after his match and sat throughout the press conference with his hands up to his face, his mouth open and a look of blind panic in his eyes. When asked how he was feeling he said, "How do I look? I'm going to take a long break."

Today also saw the end of another struggle with the departure of Marcel Proust, whose fitness was always going to tell against him in the long run, especially as his obsession with keeping the ball in play has led to longer and longer rallies which have weakened him to the point of collapse. Dali played imaginative tennis and deserved the win although he was cautioned for draping his watch over a tree after the first set.

"What's wrong with that?" he asked.

"You can't do that. It's not the way things are done, Mr. Dali. Many people were shocked."

"Shocked?" said Dali. "Dear me, I do apologize." He stood up and climbed onto the table. "I apologize for shocking people!" he cried.

He was wearing no pants.

Hannah Arendt also had her hands full with Nadezhda Mandelstam but came through in the third set. Simone de Beauvoir was rather disappointing in getting past Romania's Ana Pauker, who put up a great fight. De Beauvoir did not serve well and offered little encouragement to supporters.

The four women held a joint press conference in which they said they had agreed before their matches today that the winners, whoever they were, would refuse to play on unless Rosa Luxemburg was returned and every other player given a guarantee of safety by the tournament. De Beauvoir and Arendt both confirmed they will not play again unless the condition is met.

SuperTom did not attend the post-match press conference

after his doubles match, possibly because he didn't want to be questioned about his statement that he "didn't see the point in all this fuss about some Polish woman." Another reason advanced for his nonattendance was his wish to avoid questions about exactly what he was doing out there today. He took a casual attitude to proceedings and appeared to have no interest whatever in the result.

Groucho Marx was full of praise for his partner after the match. "I've got real admiration for these guys who have proper training. I've really got no technique. I never learned any. It's just great for me to be out here with guys like Tom."

Marx's enthusiasm for SuperTom was in evidence on the court. He ran about like a madman while Eliot waited like an Easter Island statue. Runyon and Low are a fair package at any price and will attract interest on today's showing but there was little doubt in the press box that SuperTom was conserving his energy for the singles.

A much better example was provided by Tony Chekhov, who peeled off a top-drawer singles performance to move past Wodehouse and then turned up on Court 3 with Arthur Miller to do battle in the men's doubles. What a combination this is! Miller has every shot in the book and is one of the fittest players in the game; with the general controlling the backcourt, there is little left to chance. Their opponents today, Lardner and Fitzgerald, are neighbors and friends. They were in high spirits and throughout the match they laughed and told stories and drank rather a lot of what appeared to be water from what seemed to be water bottles. They said afterwards they thought their opponents deserved to win.

"I thought they were very impressive," said Lardner.

"They were very good," agreed Fitzgerald. "Who were they?"

"I've got no idea," said Lardner.

The upset of the round in the men's doubles was the loss of Einstein and Gödel, beaten by Benchley and Thurber. Einstein's serve kept the Europeans in the contest but against two very imaginative players Gödel's lack of speed was always a problem.

Leni Riefenstahl and Mata Hari beat Margaret Mead and Freya Stark in a lively match, making rather a nonsense of Sartre's claim in this morning's paper that, "No one associated with the German tennis authorities is any good at tennis."

Hari, a Dutch doubles specialist known for her close association with the German game, did not turn up for the media conference and it was left to Riefenstahl to explain why they played in black skirts.

"There is no rule preventing us from playing in black skirts."

Had they been instructed to wear black skirts?

"Certainly not," said Riefenstahl.

Had they discussed it before the match?

"I don't recall. I don't think so."

How was it that they *both* wore black skirts?

"Coincidence," said Riefenstahl.

An hour later Riefenstahl was back out on court in a mixed-doubles match with the Austrian journeyman Hitler, who went to school with Wittgenstein and has subsequently hated Jews, Catholics, homosexuals, intellectuals, aristocrats, ascetics, teachers and all madmen above average height. Neither he nor Riefenstahl attended the press conference after their match (they went down to Freud and Klein) but presumably it was also a "coincidence" that the majority of the crowd was dressed in black shirts.

Day 26

Freud v. Matisse • Faulkner v. Robeson • Smith v. Elliott • Rhys v. Stein • Magritte v. van Gogh

"Very interesting," said Freud after his match against Matisse. "I concluded that Henri was playing in a dream."

"Here we go," said Matisse. "What sort of dream?"

"It was a dream in which you were playing tennis."

"I thought I *was* playing tennis," said Matisse.

"In the dream?" probed the Doc.

"No. Just out there. Half an hour ago."

"Of course. And were you defeating your opponent?"

"I won the first set," Matisse recalled. "And then I won the second . . ."

"Ah, but you didn't win the third, did you?" countered the Doc.

"I didn't," agreed Matisse.

"In fact you were humiliated in the third, weren't you?"

"I wouldn't say humiliated," said Matisse. "I broke a string at 5–5 and that was that."

"In this dream, what color clothing were you wearing?"

"It wasn't a dream but I was wearing white."

"Ah!" said Freud. "White. You know what that signifies, don't you?"

"That we were playing tennis?" ventured Matisse.

"Semen."

"Semen?" said Matisse. "Now we're getting somewhere. Last night I was fucking this model . . ."

"I don't want to hear about that. I want to discuss your sexual repression," said the Doc.

"That's exactly what I was saying to her!" said Matisse. "She has these particularly wonderful breasts—"

"Please," interrupted Freud.

"I mean seriously beautiful," continued Matisse. "Now, between ourselves, I'm an arse man but is there anything more beautiful than a pair of full bulging—"

"Enough already!" said Freud. "Everyone can hear you. You're talking into a microphone!"

"Correct," said Matisse with a smile. "Anyone else want me to stop?"

And, of course, as with the Frenchman's play during the match itself, nobody wanted Matisse to stop and Freud could only watch his own dream begin to evaporate.

"Sigmund has changed everything about the game," concluded Matisse. "My own opinion is that he's better at describing his conclusions than he is at reaching them."

Bill Faulkner didn't know quite how to deal with Paul Robeson. The two hadn't met before and they tested each other out for a set and a half. Robeson is a great athlete and was in excellent touch until he was informed, at two sets up, that his American passport had been revoked.

"Revoked?" he queried. "Do you mean I can't go home after the tournament?"

"That's right," said a US official.

"Can't get back into my own country? Why not?"

"Perhaps you should have thought about that before you criticized American tennis."

"Why shouldn't I criticize the way things are done in America?" asked Robeson.

"Because America is a free country. And the cost of freedom is eternal vigilance."

"How can it be a free country," asked Robeson, "if it can't be criticized by its own citizens?"

"In order for a society to work properly," explained the official, "its citizens must be opposed to its enemies."

"A society is a group of citizens who all think the same?" asked Robeson. "Could you perhaps name one?"

"Don't try to be clever. Americans are individuals. It is

in your beloved Russia that everyone is forced to think the same."

"You listen here, pipsqueak," said Robeson. "I am not here playing for America. I'm playing for the *black* people in America."

He resumed the match in a quiet fury but the incident upset his rhythm and he seemed worn out. He had come so far and a great sense of hopelessness now settled on his effort. Many in the crowd couldn't bear to look as he played out the match, magnificent at times and always with dignity but broken and disappointed. Afterwards he thanked the crowd. "A word or two before you go," he said. "I have done the state some service. And they know it."

There was also a touch of tragedy about Bessie Smith, the tall and powerful stroke-maker whose wonderful rhythm was the deciding factor in her win over Maxine Elliott. Smith said afterwards that she loved to play and especially in Paris. Elliott agreed. "It's a great thing to come from some little place somewhere and end up playing in Paris in front of all these people."

What was the particular appeal of Paris?

"It ain't St. Louis," said Smith. "Nobody knows you when you're down and out."

West Indian born but now based in England, Jean Rhys has some experience of the heat and when the humidity went through the roof early this afternoon she must have realized she had a sliver of a chance against the solid technique of Gertrude Stein. Stein is no stranger to local conditions and was well supported.

Hemingway, Picasso and Pound were all at courtside and French and American paparazzi vied with one another for position.

Stein said later it was not the heat that beat her, but the fact that she failed to vary her play. "The heat. Not the heat. The heat beat. The heat did not beat," she revealed. "The play was the same. The play that was the same beat. The beat of the play that was the same beat. It was the same. It was the same beat. The play was the same beat was the same play beat was the same."

Rhys had a different approach. "I knew something of the way Gertrude worked and I tried to imagine her as coming from the same background as myself, in Dominica. Then I could understand her and work out what she was about." She began, as it were, to think as Stein and to make Stein think as her. Rhys was in high spirits after the match.

An hour later she and Raymond Chandler were dug out of a bar in a nearby hotel and informed that their mixed-doubles match was about to start on Court 4. They had another quick one and got to the court looking slightly distracted but, the moment play got under way, you'd have thought they were the world champions. Their rhythm was superb, their placement was deadly and their stamina was admirable.

Yeats put Gershwin out of business quite early and there was some suggestion the American was burdened with an injury of some kind. "I don't know," he said. "I didn't feel too bad but I certainly couldn't lift when I needed to."

Magritte was out today too. His ability to disguise his shots was much in evidence but he could do little against van Gogh at full pace. In the third set van Gogh got an astonishing 112 percent of first serves in and ran from point to point as if working to a deadline.

"Theo told me to play my natural game," he said. "So I did. Theo is a good man."

And was he pleased with the win?

"What we need is not to win. Winning is nothing. What we need is to love."

He must nevertheless be pleased with his form?

"Form? It is not form. It is work. I hit the ball and then I run to where it will land and I hit it again. I do this until it stops coming back or until I break it."

The mystery of Rosa Luxemburg deepened late this afternoon when Osip Mandelstam vanished following his mixed-doubles match. He was due to attend a press conference with his partner but she turned up alone, forty minutes late, bruised and shaking. These occurrences cannot continue, especially at the end of a day on which the much loved American Paul Robeson was told he is not welcome in his own country. Organizers must sort it all out, and fast. They must find those responsible, remove and punish them. Security must be tightened and the players' safety guaranteed. The future, not just of the tournament but of the game, is at stake.

A shadow has fallen over proceedings. Faulkner caught the

mood of the occasion well and was torn by the instinct to exploit it and the need to help those players who are in trouble. "The impossible and the inevitable became," he said, "as they must and cannot become, the things that, at that precise moment, were required by the straining of the very moment against itself."

Day 27

Millay v. Pavlova • Tagore v. Eliot • Spock v. Joyce • Mann v. Mayakovsky • Akhmatova v. Stephen-Woolf • Duchamp v. Hemingway

What a day to finish the fourth-round singles! The victory of Edna St. Vincent Millay over Anna Pavlova has sent other players a message loud and clear. The pattern of the match was the same throughout: a fabulous display from the in-form Pavlova, followed by a brilliant tactical comeback from Millay. She came from 0–4 down to lose the first set narrowly, and from 0–3 and 0–5 down to get up in the other two. As Pavlova said in the post-match interview, "Edna played great today. I gave it everything but she was just too good. Can I thank the crowds? I love to play here. Thank you. You've been fantastic."

Millay was indeed too good on the day. "I really enjoy the doubles," she said. "I find all this singles stuff a bit of a strain."

On Court 1 we saw the Bengal tiger very nearly give a famous man a mauling. Rabindranath Tagore, who has been making his way quietly through the men's draw, is a player who can serve and volley and who can, if required, stand on the baseline and take an opponent apart with tactics. He is patient and thorough. Eliot did only what he needed to do. "He plays like an Englishman," Tagore said. "This is all very well as far as it goes. But it is not the whole story. He also plays like an American. This is the difficulty for me. I play like an Indian. We know the English but the mysteries of America are less familiar to us."

So how would Tagore tackle SuperTom in any future match-up?

"Hold the tournament in India. This is the whole problem," he said. "If we held the tournament in Delhi, the results would be completely different. Completely different. The purpose of this tournament is to establish the primacy of Western European tennis. How many Africans, Arabs and Asians are playing here? Very few indeed. Is this because of some innate incapacity among the great majority of the world's population to stand up and hit a bouncing ball? Or is it because of the way the tournament is organized?"

Surprisingly, SuperTom did turn up to today's post-match press conference although he refused to be drawn on the matter of cultural politics, or on politics more broadly or on religion, England, America, his childhood, his associations, other players, the match he had just finished, women generally and his own wife in particular, or drink. There wasn't much anyone could do about this, since Eliot is the principal editor at Laver & Laver, the licensed publisher of match reports at this tournament.

Ben Spock played sparkling tennis but was discombobulated by James Joyce, who is running into excellent form although not unencumbered by domestic problems. He dismissed these as "nothing at all" and said afterwards he had "enjoyed the match today. Young Daedalus played well and I take my hat off to him. He should get his end away tonight. Unfortunately my pleasure was impaired by the presence of a couple of spavined Carmelite tub'o'guts sitting on their gravied arses in about Row F. France is like Ireland. It's a godforsaken priest-ridden country and the sooner we learn to shit these weevils out of our system the sooner the future can begin."

Thomas Mann needed everything he could muster to get past a rather desperate Mayakovsky in a thriller. Mayakovsky's problem was that he lacked consistency. He began solidly, played spectacular tennis in the second set and struggled honestly in the third before surrendering in the fourth. Mann's ingenuity has been a feature throughout the tournament and was a telling factor again today. He rode out the storm intelligently and played the big points well.

"Pretty pleased," he said. "Mayakovsky played well and, like many others here, is monstered by the administration of the game in his own country. This is something we have to deal with, each of us. This is an international game. If we're not careful and strong, nationalism will destroy it. I am here as a German. I don't like what's happening in Germany and I can announce to you today that after this tournament I will not be returning to Germany."

So where will he live?

"Switzerland in the short term but I'm thinking of going to America. The point I want to make is that I am German, and the only way I can ensure the survival of the Germany *I* love is to leave. Mayakovsky will not have that choice. Some men in uniform took him away immediately after the match. Where is he now? Why is he not at this press conference? Is he free to say what he thinks? You people should be asking these questions."

"We're tennis reporters," said George Plimpton.

"Exactly," said Mann. "What is happening to the game you're covering? Where is Rosa Luxemburg? Where is Mayakovsky? Osip Mandelstam went missing yesterday. Where is he? His partner had been beaten up. Who did it? Robeson cannot even go back to his own country. Who are the people making these decisions? What is their purpose? What can ordinary folk do about it? What is democracy if we cannot answer these questions?"

"If we write that, our editors won't print it."

"They only want to know about the tennis," said Mailer.

"We all have families to feed."

"Of course," said Mann.

Anna Akhmatova arrived on court this afternoon despite the

best efforts of her own management. A promising junior, she was ruled out of the Russian selection process for many years and was banned altogether from playing in public. Readmitted following a change in administration at the national level she quickly emerged as one of the game's great talents. Her uneasy relationship with tennis officialdom was never more evident than it was today. She lost the first set to the intelligent play of Virginia Stephen-Woolf but when the going got tough it was Akhmatova who got going. The British press devoted more space to coverage of this match, and to Stephen-Woolf's performance here at the tournament, than to any other single player. "If the match had been between two men it would have become a classic," bellowed *The Times*.

Details of Stephen-Woolf's preparation are the subject of feature articles, often by members of her own circle. Her matches are replayed and analyzed in universities all over the English-speaking world, lists of her equipment are published on the Internet, and her laundry is for sale on eBay. Similarly, students of Russian tennis have poured out thousands of pages on the play of Akhmatova in the context of tennis, women's tennis, Russian tennis, European tennis and singles tennis.

"It didn't seem to matter what I did," said Stephen-Woolf. "Anna was awake to it and her own game is so strong it's difficult to throw her by trying to mix it up."

Did Stephen-Woolf go into the match with a plan?

"I think it's important to play your own game. Only then can you vary it. Before one can do that, however, one must develop a game of one's own. This is a great strength of Anna's too, so I needed to be careful. First I imagined myself playing as a woman, but of course Anna was already doing this very successfully, and in a sense this was my problem. Then I imagined myself playing as a man but Anna dealt with that rather well, as Isaiah Berlin had led me to believe she would. In the end I think Anna's determination to survive was perhaps greater than my own."

Akhmatova thanked Stephen-Woolf and said the other person she wanted to thank was Osip Mandelstam. "Osip and I came through the junior ranks together and he taught me a great deal. Russian tennis authorities are very efficient. They will know where Osip is and they will be proud today that so much international attention is being paid to Russian tennis. I invite you all to be here in an hour. They will bring Osip Mandelstam here. We will thank him together."

There is a powerful sense of foreboding now about where this tournament is going. The tennis and the event itself are struggling to stay in touch with one another. Some say only the tennis is real and nothing else matters. Others say the tennis is nothing; a distraction; an escape from reality. The play has been of the highest quality but there is no hiding the fact that the game faces serious problems. There is no word about the condition of Mayakovsky. Osip Mandelstam did not reappear this afternoon after a Russian official announced that he has "a hamstring problem."

Paul Robeson has declared he will travel to Russia where he will play in a series of "exhibition matches." This has been described at the American Tennis Activities Hearings as "absolute proof of exactly what we were saying, whatever it was."

"I am a black American," said Robeson. "I can do anything except go to my own country and be free."

Dmitri Shostakovich, through to the second round of the men's doubles with compatriot Prokofiev, is nowhere to be seen either. Russian officials say he is "nursing a strained shoulder."

There is still no clue to the whereabouts of Rosa Luxemburg.

Spanish customs officials announced today that Walter Benjamin, the German who played so well here earlier, had been found dead near the border. Friends say Benjamin did not want to return to Germany.

And then there was the Duchamp–Hemingway match. Hemingway arrived, unshaven but splendid after a photo shoot for *Life* magazine holding a bull scrotum between his firm white teeth. He seems to have substituted a wider public appeal for the group of private supporters who attended his earlier matches though his entourage today was somewhat depleted. Neither Agnes, Hadley, Pauline, Martha nor Mary was there. Sherwood Anderson was not there and neither were Fitzgerald, Pound and personal trainer Max Perkins. Gertrude Stein was present but seemed distracted and when she offered advice Hemingway turned to her and said, "Thank you. I'll take suggestions from people who are still in the draw."

"What are you doing?" she asked him.

"I'm exhibiting grace under pressure," he replied, "and if necessary I shall continue to do so."

"You'll have to," she replied, "if you keep playing like that."

By contrast Duchamp almost sneaked onto the court, touched his toes a couple of times and waited for his opponent to make a move. At 4–4 in the first set he hit three winners from the Hemingway serve and the crowd sensed the initial rituals in a blood sacrifice to be played out in the sun.

Round
5

Day 28

Dali v. Joyce • Matisse v. Chekhov • Akhmatova v. Bernhardt • Einstein v. Duchamp • Chandler and Hammett v. Benchley and Thurber • Leavis and Lawrence v. Chaplin and O'Neill

Salvador Dali did something today which has never been done before in open competition. He called for the official tournament doctor and asked to see a psychiatrist because, he said, he wanted to find out whether he was insane. It was halfway through the second set and he thought he could hear voices.

"Of course he can hear voices," said his opponent Joyce. "We all do. The place is full of them fifteen-love thirty-love thirty-fifteen thirty-all its like a river of peoples talk the scores the riddle of steeples torque the whores the fiddle of Jesus balk the cause the middle of deepest Cork the floors."

"Thank you," said Dali. "If you don't mind I'll go with the possibility of my own insanity."

"You're not insane," said Joyce. "You're Spanish. You come from a priest-addled slut bastard of a country like Ireland."

"I am a sex god," said Dali.

"You cannot be a god of any kind," said Joyce. "There is no God."

"I must be insane then, to imagine I am one."

"Not at all," replied Joyce. "The idea of God is used to manipulate people. That's what you're trying to do now."

"I must be insane to do that," said Dali.

"You seem to me to be as sane as the next man."

"Ah!" said Dali. "I believe that is the problem."

"What makes you sure your belief system is reliable?" asked Joyce.

"Good point," said Dali. "Get me a doctor immediately."

This was all very amusing but did little to stay the hand of fate. The combination of Joyce's court coverage and accuracy was too much on the day.

"Great shot," called Matisse as Chekhov returned the first serve of their match.

"Couldn't have put it better myself," said Mailer, in the press box.

Matisse had sent down a vicious kicker into the body. Instead of moving to the right and playing a cramped shot in defense, Chekhov had drifted left, allowed the serve to move across him and then pelted it back across court as Matisse trundled in to put away the regulation volley. It was an ominous sign. In bright sunlight in front of a packed house Chekhov played Matisse like a fish for two sets. It was impossible to imagine how the Frenchman, especially in the heat, could come back from 1–6, 2–6, 0–3.

"Wasn't looking good," said Matisse. "I felt like a blur. I was running about like a madman but Tony is so accurate there's nothing you can do when he's playing like that. Whatever happens, he turns it to his advantage."

In fact this extended even to the breaks. Chekhov plays the game at an intensity that requires intervals and he uses them brilliantly. "The intervals," he asserted, "are as important as the play."

How Matisse cut his way back into this match is anyone's guess. Exhausted and right up against it, he struggled to hold serve for 1–3 in the third and then broke Chekhov for the first time. He stopped worrying about how things looked and hit it as he felt. He sacrificed some precision but, since precision is the stock in trade of the Chekhov game, this unhorsed his opponent's approach more than it did his own. He won the next four games to take the set and took the fourth to love. Chekhov won the first two games of the final set and a man just down from the press box looked at the woman next to him as if he'd known her for years. "We're in for something here," he said.

Matisse promptly took three games on the trot and played

his best tennis of the match. As Chekhov approached his chair at the changeover, he muttered something. "I beg your pardon, Mr. Chekhov?" inquired the umpire.

Chekhov turned, the faintest smile on his lips. "I was just saying I wouldn't mind going to Moscow."

At 2–5 it looked as if the Frenchman was on his way to a quarterfinals berth. But, as so often before, Chekhov's instinct about how the play should finish was unerring. He broke Matisse twice and served it out at 7–5. Asked what he planned from here, he said, "Wasted opportunities. Less is more."

He then paused, brightened, looked as if he had had another thought and leaned into the microphone. "I was going to say something else," he said, "but I don't believe I will."

Russia's Anna Akhmatova also went through to the semifinal after beating the heroic Bernhardt in a nip-and-tuck affair. Bernhardt gave a towering performance in the first set, but the patient Akhmatova insinuated herself into the second and dictated terms in the third. Bernhardt pronounced herself "very satisfied. There are no Germans left to beat."

Akhmatova will play the winner of the Arendt–de Beauvoir contest, which has been postponed. Both players have refused to appear until the WTO "ensures Rosa Luxemburg's safety and addresses player security as a matter of urgency." Officials say they "are working through the issues and are hoping to reschedule the Arendt–de Beauvoir match in the next couple of days."

An hour after this, however, de Beauvoir turned out on Court 3 with JPS for their mixed-doubles encounter with Wilding and

Elliott, which they lost. Asked why she played, in spite of her own ultimatum, de Beauvoir replied, "Because he asked me."

"That would be right," said Nelson Algren from the players' box. "Speak like a saint. Behave like a dog on a chain."

Albert Einstein threw everything he had at Marcel Duchamp this afternoon and for over an hour we saw serving of such intensity that spectators were advised to turn their backs while the ball was being hit and then turn around quickly to see the result. In the first set Duchamp took evasive action and tried not to get hurt. Then Einstein served an ace which crashed into the metal railing around the base of a television tower and took out part of a corporate box before striking Duchamp on the wrist, smashing his watch.

"It doesn't matter," said Duchamp. "I don't need to tell the time."

"You can't anyway," said Einstein. "Time is curved. I'm sorry about the serve. I'll pull it back a bit."

"Time is curved?" protested Duchamp. "I think you'll find that's not right."

"It is right," said Einstein. "I can prove it."

"I look forward to it," said Duchamp and settled in for an explanation.

Einstein smiled. "You probably wouldn't understand the proof. It's very complicated."

"You can prove time is curved," checked Duchamp, "but I wouldn't understand the proof?"

"That's about it."

"What a shame."

"You don't think time is curved?" asked Einstein.

"Of course time isn't curved," replied Duchamp. "It's a rhombus."

"Can you prove that?" asked Einstein.

"I can," said Duchamp, "but you probably wouldn't understand it."

In the second set Einstein's serve lost some of its penetration and Duchamp began to call out, "Oh, that is art!" whenever he hit a winner. Einstein learned not to bother chasing these shots, and then after a while noticed that they weren't all winners.

"He had me completely fooled," he said later. "He was calling things 'art' that were actually just rubbish." This, of course, went to the core of the French game—whether the significance of a shot lay in the shot itself or in the way it is described. A unicorn exists because we can describe it. If Duchamp says something is art, is it art, or is Duchamp fooling us? If it is art, rubbish is art. If it is not art, who else is fooling us?

By the time Einstein addressed himself to these questions, he had let a lot of points go and the Frenchman was easing away. Einstein played with great power but was simply outfoxed.

Chandler and Hammett improvised well in a tough spot created by Benchley and Thurber. "It all happened very fast," Chandler said. "I'd heard of these guys. Word was they knew what they were doing. Word was right. Tall one could serve. The kid at the net hardly moved. Fired a few at the tall one. Got them back hard. Pinged a couple at the kid. Got them back clever.

"'You take the tall one,' growled Dash. 'Leave the other one to me. I'll meet you back at the car.'

"'Wait,' I said. 'Toss it in behind the kid. Tall guy will move across to cover, then we punch it into the gap where tall guy was.'

"'This had better work,' scowled Dash.

"'Trust me,' I said.

"'Why should I?' he barked.

"He had a point. I didn't even trust myself."

The Leavis–Lawrence combination, so strong in the first round, came apart today against Chaplin and O'Neill.

"We were great in practice," said Leavis.

"We were great in theory," corrected Lawrence.

"You played well," said Leavis.

"I played like a woman," said Lawrence.

"Just so," said Leavis. "You're at your best when you're playing like a woman."

"You played like a stick insect," said Lawrence.

"Is this irony?" asked Leavis.

"No, cunt," Lawrence assured him, "it is not fucking irony. It is an industrial strength piston-driven fact."

Day 29

Stravinsky v. Mann • van Gogh v. Orwell • Rhys v. Millay • Stead v. Smith • Waller v. Yeats • Eliot v. Wittgenstein • Lardner v. Faulkner • Auden and MacNeice v. Kafka and Muir • Sackville-West and Stephen-Woolf v. Prichard and Richardson

At the opening of the Stravinsky–Mann match, the wind swirled and eddied on court. As the gusts grew more fierce, canvas began flapping and lanyards slapped on poles. Bottles and cans rattled around in the stands.

Mann elected to serve and was waiting for a lull in the tempest when Stravinsky began running about the court with his arms spread out like wings, stamping his feet and changing direction, darting and weaving. All this movement was in perfect time with the jangling and scraping sounds, the banging of distant doors, the screeching of wire as fences strained against metal supports and dragged across uneven concrete surfaces. On and on went Stravinsky, driving himself into a fury, wheeling about in the sea of detritus.

Just as abruptly, the wind dropped, the storm abated and Stravinsky slowed in his movements until, arriving back where he had started, he folded his arms, dropped to the ground and picked up his racquet. At first a few people in the crowd applauded. Others joined them. Soon the entire stadium was clapping wildly.

"I don't even know what it was," enthused a Latvian woman, "but it was beautiful."

"Never seen anything like it," said a man from Wisconsin.

"We were beside ourselves," said a Scandinavian couple.

What the Mann from Lubeck thought of this performance was not clear, but when play began he got about his business. As with all his matches, Mann was scrutinized by German tennis officials. Their eyes followed him around the court. They waggled their fingers at him and took notes. This seemed to spur Mann on. "They drive me," he revealed. "I am really playing against them. As long as they are there, I will be playing against them."

"Vincent has a big first serve," said Orwell before their match on the court next door, "and when his ground strokes are working he generates enormous power. He gets frustrated easily, which suggests some of his battles are internal. I don't know whether Vincent plans his matches but, if he is hitting the ball well, that won't matter much. I respond to what is happening around me. Vincent is elemental. Today's question is 'can a boat beat the ocean?'"

This turned out to be a fair assessment. Van Gogh served fourteen aces in the first set and lost two games. Orwell hoisted storm cones and waited. Van Gogh served eleven aces in the second and lost five games. Orwell prepared himself but still lay low. In the third, van Gogh served fifteen aces and lost the set 1–6. Orwell was up off the canvas and, as Vangers said later, "I was hitting it well but it would not go where I wanted. I hate it when that happens."

"It was touch and go," said Orwell. "I thought I was down and out. But that's happened to me here before and I got through it."

"Can we get a drink?" asked Jean Rhys after dropping her serve for the second time in the first set against the dextrous Millay.

"A proper drink," agreed Millay. "We're not children."

"Can't play without a drink," said Rhys. "I'm here to play. I'm here *because* I play. There seems no point whatsoever in not doing it properly."

"Quite agree," said Millay.

The pair sat down to await a ruling. After conferring, officials informed the players that the beverages in the courtside fridge had been approved in accordance with regulations and sponsorship arrangements. The players were to drink them.

"I must go the toilet," said Rhys.

"Me too," said Millay. "Is that really the time?"

Suitably refreshed, the players returned and the second set featured some stupendous tennis. Both were sharper, more energetic, and their skills were on open display: Rhys out-maneuvering Millay and then moving in for the kill, the tactical Millay playing the big points superbly, building her strength to pull away in the third.

"That was great," said Rhys afterwards. "I didn't feel a thing."

"Thank God we got a heartstarter into us," agreed Millay.

"Don't mind if I do," said Rhys. "Just a small one."

And how would they describe their match?

"No idea," said Rhys. "I haven't seen it yet."

"Two slatterns and a net," said Millay.

Bessie Smith arrived late for her match against Christina Stead and had trouble hitting the ball. During the warm-up she sat down twice, and when the first game started she waited to receive service without a racquet. Stead and Darwin had a word with her and all agreed the match should be postponed. At the press call Stead acknowledged, "Bessie wasn't well. We've been rescheduled for tomorrow."

"What was wrong with her?" asked Mailer.

"No idea," said Stead.

"Was she drug-tested?"

"Any other questions?"

Fats Waller is a remarkable customer. When all this is over and the caravan moves on, a lot of people are going to realize they've never seen anything quite like him. Some will shake their heads with a smile and say, "Natural rhythm. Natural talent. Could do it in his sleep." But the more we see of Waller, the more we see of his thinking. The planning might not be obvious—today, for example, against Big Bill Yeats, he missed a lot of forehand winners in the first stanza. Time and again the ball sat up and, instead of putting it away, Waller took the pace off and just got it back in play. Later, when Yeats began to tire in the crucial fourth set, he relied on playing to Waller's muted forehand. Waller wound up and nailed winner after winner.

In the second set, with Yeats firing them in, Waller made no attempt to get his first serves back and even asked a linesman if he could borrow a chair while receiving. "If I'm going to be a spectator," he said, "I might as well sit down."

This caused great amusement but, again, there was method in it. He stood right up to the second serve and punched it low at Big Bill's feet or drove it back past him as he came in. Yeats was being told, "You must get your first serve in to win the point. Miss it, and you're in trouble." Pressure on the Yeats serve was being dressed up as admiration for the first serve. The percentage of first serves in began to drop. From 87 percent at the beginning of the set it dropped to 63 percent by the end. Waller's own game is solid and he hustles well but he won today with self-control and smart thinking.

Yeats, who rewrote the record books as a youngster, was given a standing ovation as he left. He looked older, but heads still turn when something magnificent walks by.

When Eliot met Wittgenstein (not a bad title for a film) and they were tossing before their match, SuperTom was diffident and Wittgenstein was guarded. Eliot had heard so much about this opponent and had seen him, in practice, taking apart the sort of game he himself had spent years developing. His serve-and-volley approach would be put under serious examination and might well be shredded. For SuperTom to stay on the baseline and try to slug it out would be to flirt with catastrophe.

Wittgenstein looked at Eliot and asked him whether he would like to serve.

"But you won the toss," protested SuperTom.

"The toss is nothing," said Wittgenstein. "I'm seeking your preference because I do not have one."

"I don't know that I have one either," replied SuperTom.

"Not knowing you do is not the same as knowing you do not."

"I don't dispute that."

"Not disputing it," said Wittgenstein, "is not the same as agreeing with it."

"Jug, jug, jug, jug," said SuperTom, "*la plume de ma* time and death."

"Thought so," said Wittgenstein. "You serve."

"I am not Prince Hamlet," said SuperTom. "Nor was meant to serve."

"Which end do you want?" asked Wittgenstein.

"End?" queried SuperTom. "Maybe drowning."

The match had a similarly disjointed character, on top of which, at 3–2 in the second set, Wittgenstein noticed Karl Popper in the stand and shook his racquet at him. "Bugger off!" he advised.

"Ah!" Popper called to the crowd. "Aggression! Did you see that? He threatened me!"

"Sit down, you twerp," said Wittgenstein.

"Twit twit twit," said SuperTom.

"Good man," said Wittgenstein and relaxed his grip on the matter. His concentration in the next two sets was astonishing. He hardly looked up, muttered to himself constantly and paid no attention to the scoreboard. Then, at 3–0 up in the final set, he apologized to Eliot and said he "had completely misunderstood the question."

At 3:45 this afternoon Ring Lardner became the longest priced quarterfinalist anyone in the press box could remember. He beat Bill Faulkner in four, disguising his game craftily and allowing Faulkner to think he had it won until the last. "I was strong at the beginning," Faulkner asseverated, "and, following the beginning was, persistently (yes) strong in that section beyond the beginning but not yet in the middle and then, when the middle, as it must, by virtue of its being the middle, without which there would be no ends, arrived, I was persistent there in my strength also. But at the last it was he, rather than

I, who reached out and took the match. I persisted. He persisted. We persast."

Auden and MacNeice then destroyed Kafka and Muir in an unparalleled demonstration of doubles play. Kafka was in sparkling form and Muir is solid in all passages, but Auden and MacNeice sometimes play like a single organism and today it was impossible to put anything between them. With the Auden serve on fire and MacNeice, proprietor of one of the best backhands in the game, elegant and deadly, they didn't miss much.

Another great combination went through on Court 4, where Sackville-West and Stephen-Woolf, who have been playing together since they were both girls, got home despite a nasty scare. Prichard and Richardson took the first set before their more fancied opponents, who seemed rather to be hibernating, emerged into the full light of day.

Sackville-West and Stephen-Woolf play in long dresses and cardigans. They speak only to people to whom they have been formally introduced, which was a bit trying for the umpire today, ignored for two sets and then instructed to "sit down you ridiculous little thing. If we want anything, we'll ring." Their play is imperious and they sometimes behave as if their opponents aren't there.

"We assume there is some opposition," explained Sackville-West. "A view confirmed on this occasion by the fact that so many of the balls we hit were in fact returned."

"We're not idiots," added Stephen-Woolf. "There was manifestly some human agency involved."

With their peculiar birdlike movements, they presented a commendable spectacle. Their understanding of one another was practically psychic in the third set, when Richardson, serving superbly, was shut out by a refusal to acknowledge that it was happening. The faster the serves got, the faster the returns came back.

Day 30

Stead v. Smith • Sartre and Camus v. Magritte and Dali • Nijinsky and Pavlova v. Bankhead and partner • Shostakovich and Prokofiev v. Cocteau and Picasso

Schwarztag.

Rosa Luxemburg is dead.

Her body was found in an industrial estate at dawn this morning. She had been shot at close range. This tragedy, on top of the murder of Karl Liebnecht, the suicide of Walter Benjamin and the disappearance of Osip Mandelstam, has thrown the future of the tournament into serious doubt. WTO organizers had undertaken to provide assurances by tonight that there would be no further incidents of this kind. No such undertaking has been received.

All flags are flying at half mast. The tournament has expressed its "profound sorrow" to Ms. Luxemburg's family and has issued a statement: "A decision will be made tonight or early tomorrow concerning the schedule for the remaining matches."

There has been some criticism of the WTO's handling of this issue. Auden, for example, said he had a feeling this might happen and it is not yet clear what, if anything, tournament management did to prevent it.

"We're running a tennis tournament," said one official. "We're not responsible for everything that happens to individual competitors."

"Nobody said you were," replied Auden. "The question is, who is responsible for the death of Luxemburg?"

"Not us."

"Then who?" asked Auden.

"The players are responsible for themselves. They're all capable adults."

"Is Rosa Luxemburg to blame for her own death?" Auden persisted. "Did she shoot herself six times in the back of the head from a distance of two meters?"

"We don't know what precisely happened to player Luxemburg," said the official.

"Why don't you know? You're the WTO."

"Perhaps, out of respect," said the official, "we should not engage in speculation about what is a tragic matter."

"It is quite clear she was killed by her own people," said Auden.

"Not by herself. Not by people who did not know who she was. It's not a mystery. By doing nothing, the tournament is complicit in her murder."

"I thought you were going to America," said the official.

"I do not wish to go to the America you come from," said Auden,

> "You do not realize you will go to the limestone I come from.
> Where I arrive, you will be free to talk rubbish.
> When you return, I will be prevented from talking sense.
> In your new empire, strength will shoot craps with paranoia.
> In my old age, memory will change hats with impunity.
> You would like nothing more than to see me wish upon a star.
> I would like to see you fired into another galaxy.
> Unless you are very careful, your utopia will run out of gas.
> Unless I am much mistaken, my dinner will be in the oven."

"You are obtuse," said the official. "And you go on too much."

"Tennis makes nothing happen," Auden went on,

> "Indifferent in a month,
> Rankings are just a lot of bumpf.
> Obsession with winning and making a packet,
> Rebounds from every tennis racquet."

Arthur Miller, still in the doubles with Chekhov and looking at a great future in the game, was also resolute. "Unwilling or unable to control the German or Russian federations, the WTO must broker an arrangement which allows the tournament to continue. It must do this by tomorrow and to the satisfaction of the players."

"And," agreed Mary McCarthy, "we don't just want some sordid deal between imposters and criminals. Countries like my own must ensure that they don't appease Germany and Russia for the moment but create a bigger problem later on."

"And if they negotiate in only their own interest," insisted Miller, "what difference will exist between them and the system they are replacing?"

In their rescheduled match, Christina Stead played like a woman who loved her tennis for a set and a half, until Smith's languid rhythm began to work like a slow-acting opiate to dull the sharpness of the Australian's attack. The match was stopped briefly while a young black man was removed from a tree just outside the fence at Court 4, where he seemed to be hanging to get a better view.

"I'll be back," said Smith, and left the court.

"Where are you going, Ms. Smith?" asked Charles Darwin.

"Black man hanging from a tree," she said. "I'm going to need some medicine."

"It had better be legal," said Darwin.

"Black man hanging from a tree legal?"

"I'm advising you not to take anything which is not prescribed."

" 'Taint nobody's business if I do," wailed Smith. "Feel that heat. Ain't that some heat?"

The dead man was cut down and play restarted after about twenty minutes. It was by this stage a joyless affair, however, and neither woman seemed much interested in the result. Smith went on to win but later complained of illness and was taken to the American hospital.

The men's doubles match between Sartre–Camus and Magritte–Dali had already started when the Luxemburg story broke. The umpire had to call the players together and tell them the news.

"All right," said Sartre. "Let's start again."

"Play has been called off. It's not a question of starting again. Mr. Camus, please stop bouncing the ball. Have some consideration for the dead."

"The dead?" said Camus. "The dead are dead. Let's have some fun."

"Camus is right," said JPS. "Although I forget why."

"What do your opponents think?" asked the umpire.

The group looked around and saw Magritte facing the other way with a view of the Algarve where his head should be and Dali sitting upside down with a cigarette holder running down his leg.

"I believe they support the mood of the meeting," said Camus.

"I disagree," said the umpire. "And I will suspend play forthwith."

"Play is already suspended," said Magritte. "I suspended it years ago."

"That is absurd."

"Have you ever seen play more suspended?" asked Magritte, who was now a meter above the ground and there were twelve of him.

"I suspend play immediately," insisted the umpire.

"Good on you," called Magritte, "they'll all be doing it now."

"This is completely meaningless," said the umpire.

"My point," said Camus.

"And mine to a degree," said Sartre.

"To what degree?"

"A doctorate ideally," opined Sartre. "Sorbonne would be good."

"My cock is a wealthy man," contributed Dali. "And it has made an attractive offer for my hand in marriage."

Nijinsky and Pavlova forfeited their doubles match when, during a practice session this morning, he attempted to float off a building. "Mr. Nijinsky is not well," said an official, "and, in his own interests and those of his family, he must withdraw."

"I will win the tournament," said Nijinsky. "I am God."

Shostakovich and Prokofiev had their doubles match against Cocteau and Picasso postponed because, as Prokofiev put it, "I don't know where Shosters is."

Amelia Earhart is also missing. "No one knows where she went," said a friend. "She just took off."

Some players have already left Paris. Others are packing. Wodehouse and Isherwood have departed for the US. Einstein left yesterday, last night and again this morning. Freud and Klein are still in the tournament but are wait listed. Auden and his wife are expected to go before the week is out.

"Why should Mandelstam have to forfeit her doubles match because she isn't here?" complained Helen Keller and Anne Sullivan. "Her husband has gone missing! Is she supposed to fill in time playing tennis while she waits for him to turn up? We weren't even consulted. We were just told we were through to the next round."

Peggy Guggenheim agreed. "Sam and I were told we were through in the mixed too; that the Mandelstams had forfeited. How do they know? She's frantic and he isn't even here. I'll be out buying paintings, incidentally."

It was a relief when Shostakovich turned up. It is fair to say he was pale as he read from two statements. "I damn the monstrous opinions of the fascist Russian Tennis Federation. The crimes that are committed in its name and by its agency are legion. The degradation of the human condition in Russian tennis is both pitiful and perfidious." He shuffled his pages. "I wish to make a complete apology. I know that the Russian Tennis Federation is right. I accept stern criticism and must do more to reflect glory on Russian tennis administrators, who are towering geniuses."

American team management was in damage control late today too. Bessie Smith never made it to the hospital. Unfortunately, due to what was described by medical authorities as "a mixup involving epidermal melanocytes and pigmentation," Ms. Smith was refused admission. She died in the ambulance. It was a dark coda to a tragic day.

Quarterfinals

Day 31

Shostakovich and Prokofiev v. Cocteau and Picasso
• Arendt v. de Beauvoir

This morning a meeting was held between WTO officials and players' representatives. All the day's remaining matches were postponed to allow competitors to attend funeral services. This follows crisis talks, which began last night, aimed at securing the completion of the tournament and ensuring the safety of players. The WTO "recognizes this as a priority and has tightened security at entrances and exits." The tennis federations of all playing nations have released a signed joint statement "deploring the recent tragic events in Paris" and "undertaking to meet to formulate new and binding guidelines for the conduct of future tournaments."

Matches not finished yesterday were rescheduled for this afternoon and, despite some rain, were completed.

Magritte and Dali offered to assist organizers by finishing their match against Sartre and Camus, and playing their quarterfinal against Chaplin and O'Neill, at the same time.

"Two players up one end and four up the other?"

"That's right," said Dali. "Save wear and tear on the schedule."

"But we don't know you're even in the quarterfinals yet," said Darwin. "You can't play your quarterfinal match until you beat Sartre and Camus."

"We could make it a rule that, after each serve, we hit to them first, and only hit it to Chaplin and O'Neill after JPS and Albert have had a lash at it."

"The point is, at this stage, you cannot play Chaplin and O'Neill at all."

"In that case," said Magritte, "put them up the same end as Dali and me and we'll all have a go at Sartre and Camus."

"You don't understand," said Darwin. "It has not yet been determined who will play Chaplin and O'Neill."

"Do you agree that there are only four people in the world who can possibly play Chaplin and O'Neill in the quarters?" asked Magritte. "JPS and Albert and Dali and me."

"That is exactly the position."

"Perfect," said Magritte. "Chaplin and O'Neill up one end. JPS and Albert and Dali and me up the other."

"No."

"Wasted opportunity," warned Dali.

"Doesn't make any sense at all," agreed Magritte.

In the event, Sartre and Camus took the first set but the rest of the match was a Magritte–Dali exhibition and the Belgian–Spanish combo will go on to meet Chaplin and O'Neill in the quarters.

Shostakovich and Prokofiev began well against Cocteau and Picasso but their play became erratic when they attempted to avoid the fluency of Picasso by concentrating their effort on his partner. But there's not much Cocteau can't do and it wasn't long before they were hitting the ball to Picasso to give themselves time to think. The wiry Frenchman had a field day at the net, poaching anything he could put away, sure in the knowledge that the wonderful Spaniard was taking care of business behind him.

"I had a great time," he said to the press. "I enjoy doubles, Picasso is my friend and I love this surface."

The Arendt–de Beauvoir match, much hyped by local media, was a disappointment. Arendt had come so far, but surely she couldn't topple the player for whom the women's draw seemed to have been invented. De Beauvoir said she felt great; she was fit, she was ready and she was cheered onto the court as if she were Joan of Arc's sister. Not much more than an hour earlier Sartre and Camus had been knocked over in the men's doubles, and nothing sharpens the de Beauvoir game more than a setback to JPS. The auguries had all been attended to.

The first set lasted thirty-four minutes, Arendt breaking serve at 3–3 and holding the break. In the second set de Beauvoir lost some of her focus. She missed a lot of shots wide and she double-faulted to lose her serve at 4–4. She broke back immediately with some courageous net play but Arendt was not to be denied and came back again, winning the match with three glorious forehands, two down the line and one across court, to complete a stunning anticlimax.

"I had a match plan," explained de Beauvoir, "and I followed it. The plan was worked out by my coach, based on how we thought we could win, and my job was simply to put the plan into action."

"Here was this great woman," said Arendt. "A woman who has assumed legendary status in our minds, in whom we have invested ideas and characteristics of our own, for our own reasons. And here she was now, on her own, a person like anyone else. It was, in the end, a perfectly ordinary tennis match."

What had Arendt expected?

"It wasn't just me," she said. "It was everyone. We expected something bigger, something mythic; Roman perhaps, Greek, I don't know. I don't think the reality was disappointing. She was an individual, doing her job."

"She was full of shit," said Nelson Algren from the players' box.

There was further criticism of the plan to clean up the game. "The WTO is weak," Mary McCarthy told the French media.

"If the central governing body is weak, ambitious member federations will do what they want. The rules need to be clear and they need to be policed. It's no use waiting for a problem to fester and then trying to put a bandage on it."

Others think the tournament has revealed what is going on in some of the member federations but that little can be done about it.

"It's hopeless," said Strindberg. "Hopeless and completely pointless."

"It's not hopeless," said Heidegger. "It's also none of the WTO's affair. German tennis is as good as any tennis in the world. A lot of this is jealousy."

"A lot of *what* is jealousy?"

"I forget," said Heidegger, "but I'm sure I'm right."

Roland Barthes thought these questions were irrelevant. "The significant thing is not that tennis was hijacked by totalitarianism," he said, "but that it has survived. Look at the players who are left in the draw. The only Germans left in the singles are Mann, a stalwart critic of the German administration, and Hannah Arendt, who has left the country. The only Russians are Chekhov and Anna Akhmatova, the most subtle articulator of the Russian malaise and the great surviving dissident."

He wasn't finished. "The only Americans are Waller, who isn't even allowed in certain toilets in America, Lardner, whose son has just appeared before the House American Tennis Unhearings and SuperTom, who lives in England. The only

Englishman left is Orwell, who has never even been approached to play Davis Cup and lives on an island off the coast of Scotland."

The other two are Joyce, whose matches are not allowed to be broadcast in Ireland, despite the fact that they are full of meticulously assembled shots he remembers having seen there as a child, and Duchamp, the mocker of everything French tennis stands for.

Day 32

Lardner v. Duchamp • Mann v. Eliot • Auden and MacNeice v. Chandler and Hammett • Astaire and Rogers v. Wilding and Elliott • Freud and Klein v. Beckett and Guggenheim

Chekhov and Duchamp have tough assignments in the next few days, with singles and doubles commitments. So too do doubles partners Arendt and Akhmatova in action against each other on Friday for the right to play Millay in the women's singles final.

Also busy with doubles are Beckett, Maxine Elliott and Katherine Mansfield, and all three are still in the mixed.

The first of the men's quarterfinals pitted Lardner against Marcel Duchamp. Both are capable of beating anyone. To get here, Lardner has knocked out the moody Glenn Miller, Nabokov in straight sets, Chaplin in the upset of the round, Ted Cummings and the Mississippi mauler, Bill Faulkner.

Lardner has been the underdog in every match he has played and has attracted only passing attention from the media—he used to be a sportswriter "until I found out how it worked"—but his results tell their own story. No one has taken him to five sets. He has a gift for picking a flaw in an opponent's game and there is a cruel streak in the way he exploits it. If Duchamp reveals a weakness, he will never hear the end of it.

Duchamp himself has had a tough campaign: Milne, a match he said privately he thought he might winnie in threeie, Isherwood, Mandelstam in what was probably the match of the third round, and Ernie Hemingway in the fourth. His undermining of fourth-seeded Einstein was a study in planning and execution and was replayed around the world.

Nevertheless, the Lardner–Duchamp quarterfinal featured the two players least known to the broader sporting public.

In the first set they tested one another. Lardner served powerfully and hit drives deep to both corners. Duchamp watched like a hawk and probed the sidelines, stretching the American and punching away the volley. Lardner 6–4.

The second set was all Lardner. The high-octane serve was screaming in and Duchamp sliced the returns to slow the game down. This was just what the doctor ordered as far as Lardner was concerned and he was there like a cat, hitting winner after winner. Lardner 6–4, 6–3.

The crowd could see the writing on the wall and paid no particular attention when Duchamp eased his way into the third set and won it in a tie-break with three superb lobs which had Lardner out of position and going the wrong way. Lardner 6–4, 6–3, 6–7.

The fourth set also went to a tie-break. Lardner jogged on the spot, took a couple of deep breaths and went for the kill. He stepped the serve up another notch and was deadly at the net. But Duchamp got everything back and stood his ground, winning the tie-break once again, again with three superb lobs. Lardner could only stand and watch as they drifted into the unguarded backcourt. All square, Lardner v. Duchamp 6–4, 6–3, 6–7, 6–7. The crowd lifted. Duchamp allowed himself a wry smile but knew there was work still to do.

Twenty-seven minutes later that work was done. Game, set and match Duchamp, 4–6, 3–6, 7–6, 7–6, 6–2.

The Mann–Eliot encounter was a different affair altogether. Both players expected to be in the quarters and each knows the other's game. They are strong and uncompromising men and had taken some bruising to get here. Mann was lucky to get past Kandinsky, Eisenstein, Satie and Mayakovsky but then had surprisingly little trouble with Stravinsky. SuperTom began with routine wins against Capek and Crosby but then ran into Shaw in a grudge match which nearly upset the applecart. Tagore and then Wittgenstein took more out of the Eliot legs and it was a battle-hardened SuperTom who stepped out on Centre Court today.

This would be big, powerful stuff. There would be a lot of noise and one man would not get up. The gods were angry.

Mann blinked in the first set and lost it 6–4. SuperTom blinked in the second and lost it 7–5. The Mann service quickened in the third and he took it 6–3. Mann had set his sail and was heading for open sea.

SuperTom pretended it was all in a day's work but he looked like a country vicar who'd found himself in charge at Passchendaele. He hadn't done much wrong, but here he was in full retreat in a battle controlled by someone else. He needed to break out. Could he do it? Did he dare?

"It was time," he said later. "I decided to fight the fact that fire was being fought with fire, with fire."

There was extra bite in the SuperTom serve in the fourth quartet. His ground strokes were low and hard, and anything Mann lobbed was murdered. Mann defended his lead and slowed the game down but this simply highlighted SuperTom's gift for setting up well-constructed points. He broke Mann twice and took the match to a fifth set.

SuperTom was back in town. When Eliot is running hot he can do anything; the power game is huge, he disguises his intentions well and even scraps of shots become part of a seamless cloth.

It was well known that Auden planned to leave town as soon as possible but today he and MacNeice played as if they wanted to stay here forever, and at times had this match at their mercy.

Chandler and Hammett, however, were not about to lie down.

"Can't afford to lie down in this business," said Chandler. "Down the other end were two guys. Same as last time. Different guys. Same deal. Big one looked like a hangover with the lot but the other one was slick, like a fish with a good barber. Maybe he deals a little insurance to widows and maybe a little something else besides.

"I opened the courtside fridge and got a message from my nerves demanding to know where they kept the whiskey and could we go home soon. A flatfoot sitting up a ladder somewhere said, 'Play.' I thought of looking up but my eyes had been on strike for better pay and conditions and I didn't want to inflame the issue.

"Dash and I lost the first set. The hangover was packing plenty of punch and the insurance man was picking up work all over town.

"'Do these guys know something we don't?' asked Dash as we sat down.

"'My feet hurt,' I said.

"'They're just a couple of punks,' said Dash.

"'I think my arm is broken.'

"'Something doesn't fit,' said Dash. 'Couple of punks beating tough guys like us.'

"'There's got to be an easier way to get a thirst.'

"Dash took a long pull on his drink, threw his towel down and we went back out there. Dash isn't a big guy and he only trains nights. But don't get him angry. He fights above his weight."

The second set saw Hammett unleash himself and Auden's habit of coming across MacNeice at the net began to open gaps behind them, gaps which the intelligent Chandler saw and used. Chandler and Hammett had survived. From there, it was a short ride home.

In the first set against Anthony Wilding and Maxine Elliott in a mixed quarterfinal on Court 2, Fred Astaire and Ginger Rogers were tentative, but as light rain fell and everyone scampered under umbrellas, they seemed to get things together. When they came back out again they were superb; Astaire very much the ideas man, with Rogers moving backwards a lot to cover him. If they carry on as they did today, Fred and Ginger are going to be hard to stop.

"Isn't it a lovely day," said Astaire, "to be caught in a storm."

In the other mixed quarter today, the Austrian pairing of Freud and Melanie Klein took out Beckett and Peggy Guggenheim. Freud developed the idea that Guggenheim's habit of buying works of art by other players in the tournament was a response to having seen her parents in the act of congress.

"Oh dear," said Guggenheim. "Can we just get on with the match?"

"It's obvious," said the Doc. "The paintings are on canvas. They cover the canvas just as our conscious masks our subconscious. But the canvas they hide is white, the color of sperm."

"You could make anything fit that argument," said Guggenheim.

"Canvas isn't white, incidentally, it's a hessian color which has gesso-ground put on it and is then painted white."

"What color is it after it's been painted white?" trumpeted Freud.

"Furthermore, I had a very unsuccessful nose job so I appreciate beauty which is outside myself, my father was lost on the *Titanic* so I'm keen on things that will last, and I'm rich, so if I don't buy paintings from other players, who will?"

"This breast is on my forehand side and is good," Klein announced. "This other breast is on my backhand side and is not good."

Beckett said nothing but clearly wished the matter could be over at the earliest available opportunity and made every effort to ensure that it was.

Day 33

Waller v. Orwell • Chekhov v. Joyce • Lenya and Dietrich v. Gonne-MacBride and Markievicz • Elliott and Draper v. Sackville-West and Stephen-Woolf • Keller and Sullivan v. Akhmatova and Arendt

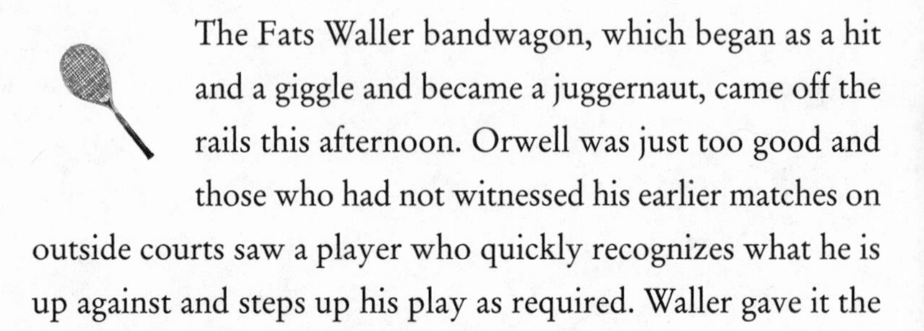

The Fats Waller bandwagon, which began as a hit and a giggle and became a juggernaut, came off the rails this afternoon. Orwell was just too good and those who had not witnessed his earlier matches on outside courts saw a player who quickly recognizes what he is up against and steps up his play as required. Waller gave it the works today, but he made no impression on Orwell.

"Had a great time here," said Fats. "Want to thank you. You've been a wonderful audience."

"I love the way that guy plays," said Orwell. "I wish I could play like that. That is the way I would like to play."

"But you must be happy," opined Plimpton of the *Paris Review*. "You won. You're into the semifinal."

"Happy? I beat a guy in Burma once, in the All-of-England-Burma-Colonial-Police-White-People-Must-Win Tennis Tournament. I don't know who was more humiliated, him or me."

There was not an empty seat at the Chekhov–Joyce quarter-final. The two heavyweights, seeded one and five, have met twice before, with honors being shared. Joyce has made no secret of his admiration for the brilliant Russian, referring to him as "the blessed St. Anton" and attributing his own early successes to the playing of Chekhov.

Just watching these two hit up was exciting. There was the Chekhov forehand, easy and strong and so variable it almost has a volume knob. And Joyce's backhand, assured, deep and with plenty of action on it.

The first set was towering stuff from the Russian. His service didn't look like being broken and he left nothing in the bag with the ground strokes. Joyce was having trouble with his glasses and before the second set he paced out the distance between the side edge of the court and the stands, because, he said, he couldn't see it properly and was going to have to remember it.

The second set saw Chekhov consolidating his position, breaking Joyce at 3-all and holding on to the break. When the set finished Joyce asked for the wind velocity to be measured. He could feel a breeze, he said, but he couldn't see the flags clearly and he needed to know what it was doing so he could remember it. Chekhov was well in front but Joyce had moved him around a lot and in the third set the Russian started to tire. Loose shots began to creep in. Easy volleys were netted. He took longer to serve and he walked around behind the baseline between points. By the time Joyce had taken the third set it was obvious Chekhov was in trouble. Joyce asked if he was OK. He was fine, he replied, although he was considering the possibility of going to Moscow.

In the fourth set Joyce produced one of the most remarkable passages of the tournament. He played to the Chekhov forehand he knows so well, and began hitting crosscourt winners from outside the sidelines and creating angles the crowd sometimes didn't believe. What we were seeing wasn't just powerful. It was new and perfect.

By the end of the set Chekhov was run ragged and his doctor came on court. Although he waved the doctor away and insisted on continuing, it wasn't surprising to hear later that he had been nursing a serious respiratory problem. Joyce took the fifth set and the match but concern was all for Chekhov. There was sustained applause as he gathered his racquets. He smiled, shook hands with Joyce and patted him on the shoulder.

"I didn't lose today because I wasn't fit," said Chekhov later. "I lost because Jim played so brilliantly. I didn't have breathing troubles in my earlier matches and I didn't have them in the first two sets today. In my view Jim's going to rewrite the book."

"What is it," inquired Barthes, "that makes Joyce different from the others?"

"He's got music," said Chekhov.

Joyce went to see an ophthalmologist after the match and was unavailable for comment.

Lenya and Dietrich beat Gonne-MacBride and Markievicz in a women's doubles match, although just beforehand it was revealed that Gonne-MacBride's husband had recently been shot "as a result of an incident involving a post office," and Markievicz acknowleged she was to be arrested as soon as she returned to Dublin. Asked if they would like the match to be postponed, the Irish women said, "No. The tennis is great. At least it has an element of chance."

Dietrich has a huge following among young American men and photographs of her are in constant circulation on the Internet even though she has never won an individual event of any kind. She was signing autographs long after everyone else had left.

Maxine Elliott was back on court again today with Ruth Draper, up against Sackville-West and Stephen-Woolf in their quarterfinal match. "It's OK," said Elliott, "I'm used to playing in the afternoon and then again at night, and so is Ruth. This is what we do."

Sackville-West and Stephen-Woolf arrived late and instructed a doorman to bring their racquets in and place them near their chairs. "Within reasonable reach," said Sackville-West, "like tools in a garden shed." They acknowledged their friends in the crowd, did a few deep knee bends and gave the signal to the umpire that the hit-up could commence. They were mightily affronted when they lost the first set, flew about like caped crusaders to win the second and, even though Sackville-West went off the boil in the third, Draper and Elliott could not stop laughing at some private joke and the English pairing took it 7–5.

There were surprises ranging from mild to extreme in the other women's doubles matches. The New Zealanders Mansfield and Hodgkins took out de Valois and Pavlova and, in an upset that must rank with the fate of Mr. Dumpty, Helen Keller and Annie Sullivan beat Akhmatova and Arendt. The two Europeans made no attempt to conserve energy before their women's singles semifinal tomorrow. They gave it everything and were in strife all the way. Part of their problem was working out who was in charge at the other end. Keller and Sullivan communicate like no one else, using words, signs and anything else they can find. With Sullivan yelling, "Helen. Backhand. Topspin. Now!" to Keller who couldn't see where the ball had landed, and Keller pointing to Sullivan to go down the tramlines, it was impossible to assess their match plan. Keller was even cautioned for calling "Yours!" to the umpire as an unplayable Akhmatova serve scorched by.

"It was a shambles," said Sullivan. "We didn't really have a plan. We just wanted to see if we could do it, I suppose."

Semifinals

Day 34

Duchamp v. Orwell • Joyce v. Eliot • Beckett and Duchamp v. Braque and Derain • Magritte and Dali v. Chaplin and O'Neill • Chekhov and Miller v. Cocteau and Picasso

The first man through to the singles final would be French or English. It was a battle sanctioned by history. Neither Duchamp nor Orwell is a big powerful player, neither has a huge serve and neither is a dominator.

If this were happening at a velodrome they would both sit high up on the bank, immobile, balancing on the pedals, each watching, waiting for the other to make a move, and then pouncing. This is sprinter behavior, but it also entails a capacity for endurance, for patience, and for being right in the long run.

Duchamp had more patience in the first set. He waited and he planned and he thought. Orwell bolted at 5–5 and Duchamp smiled slightly, knowing the set was lost but the trap was in place. In the second, Orwell sprinted earlier, winning it 6–3. Duchamp had a twinkle in his eye as he sat down and he took no drink. He was on court waiting for Orwell to begin the third and now he played like a mind reader. Wherever Orwell went, he found it covered. Whatever he tried to set up, he found it blocked. Whenever he took a risk, he was punished.

In the fourth set Duchamp built an attack designed to neutralize Orwell and stop him from creating opportunities. Part of Duchamp's strategy was to take the sting out of Orwell by getting him to accept the possibility of a draw. The Frenchman made no effort to win some points and took others easily. When he "accidentally" broke serve to take the set, Orwell realized he had been duped. Furious, he served faster in the fifth than at any time in the tournament. Although this heightened the likelihood of what he called "Double fault" (the idea that a player who is serving a lot of aces can convince himself he is winning a match he is, in fact, losing), he controlled it admirably and Duchamp's endgame began to come apart in his hands. The attack was mounted faster than it could be dismantled and Orwell went through to the final, with a chance to be the last man in Europe.

Joyce and Eliot arrived on court for their match at 2:15 p.m. Three hours later they were still out there. It was clear from the start that Eliot had never encountered anything like Joyce before, and that he didn't much like what he saw—a man whose playing gear was old and faded, whose glasses were held together with electrical tape and who was wearing borrowed shoes.

Joyce took the first before Eliot worked out quite what he was doing. As the players sat between ends, Eliot drew the umpire's attention to "a number of crude remarks" Joyce made to friends in the crowd, which SuperTom thought "brought the game into disrepute."

"Disrepute, is it?" said Joyce. "Disrepute? Do you think arseholes shooting their own players is bringing the game into repute? Do you think that, Tom? You think not letting Robeson back into Americky is good for the game, do you? Bessie Smith dying in an ambulance? That's a good result is it, Tom?"

"Joyce, please," admonished the umpire. "Not today. On this of all days."

The Irishman continued, "I'll tell you something for nothing, Tom—"

"Please, no," said the umpire. "Can we just this once not have any unpleasantness."

"You're an alleycat, Joyce," snapped SuperTom. "Rough and dirty and spraying your stink everywhere."

"Christ, you're elegant," smiled Joyce. "So fucking intelligent."

"Have you any awareness whatever of what constitutes acceptable on-court language?" asked Eliot.

"You're a great man for the pomp and circuspants, Tom. Have you had a woman lately?"

"Really," insisted the umpire. "Joyce, can you just play the game?"

"I'll not be told how to express myself by a fucking sermonizing misogynist eunuch," said Joyce.

"Drivel from a fool!" spat SuperTom.

"Or is it not really the women you're after, Tom? Is it the lads that steam the engine up?"

The height of SuperTom's dudgeon at this point was inestimable. He walked away and stood on the service line, waiting. Joyce wiped his nose on his shirt and sauntered out to receive. SuperTom served like a man who knew he was playing in a classic and won the second set going away. The third was a seesawing affair in which Eliot moved away again to a 6–4 win.

If Joyce was concerned, he didn't show it. He was still talking to people in the crowd and at 2–3 in the fourth he approached a woman about two rows back and borrowed money to continue.

In the fourth set, he talked nonstop. SuperTom bristled. He walked to the net and stared at Joyce for nearly a minute.

Joyce looked up. "How are you going, Tom?" he asked. "I'm putting a new grip on my racquet."

Joyce finished winding on the new grip but Eliot hadn't moved.

"Time, Mr. Eliot," said the umpire. "Hurry along, please. It's time."

Eliot stood at the net, rolling up the legs on his shorts.

"I am Lazarus," he said, "come back from the dead."

"And I am Molly," said Joyce, "come back from Blazes."

"Time please, Mr. Eliot."

When play restarted, Joyce carried on and the stream of his words continued, not loud enough for the umpire to take any action. In fact, it was rather mellifluous. His tennis was now moving at the pace of his voice and he was "in the zone." He won seven straight games to take the fourth set and to break Eliot in the first game of the decider.

Eliot was now cautioned for banging his racquet on the ground and yelling "Jug, jug, jug, fucking juuuuuuggggg!"

He walked to the net and glared balefully at Joyce again. "Can you keep the interior monologue down?"

"Tell me a tale of Jim and Tom," hummed Joyce to himself, "all of the river is flowing Jim, the river is flowing over him, the rivering under the floater Tom, the blow to just under the nose is gone, and into the afterglow is on, and go with the afterburners on, and go with the flow from here to there, and go with it knowing your man Flaubert, and everythings fine and Dante there, and then as you hit the final straight, you hammer it down the line and wait, and look at the time and consummate."

"I haven't been playing well, of late," said Eliot. "Teller 3 is now available, incidentally. I'm afraid you have insufficient funds in this account."

"I beg your pardon?" asked the umpire.

"Step this way please," said SuperTom. "I think we'd better see the manager."

"I am the manager," said the umpire.

"Very good," said Eliot. "Carry on."

Joyce was untroubled from here and served the match out to a great reception on all sides.

Edna St. Vincent Millay was in the crowd today to see the Beckett and Duchamp and Braque and Derain match. Duchamp had completed his singles match and must have wished it would all go away but he and Beckett are exemplars of the "doing-only-what-you-need-to-do" approach and it got them through. Braque and Derain are both strong, attacking players with good ground strokes and plenty of angles. Beckett and Duchamp rotated at the net and never let their opponents settle. The players were in high spirits at the press conference and wished it known that they always knew B and D were going to beat B and D.

Philip Rahv and Mary McCarthy took the first set against Tallulah Bankhead and her current partner but from there it was all the Bankhead pairing. Whether or not her partner today was the young man with whom she performed so spectacularly in the first round against Hammett and Hellman was not known. She herself was not saying. "I would have to check my records," she confided to the garrulous young man from *Paris-Match*, "and in order to do that I would have to have some interest in keeping records which, I can reveal to you privately, is not the case. What's your name?"

"Gervase," said the young man. "You don't keep records?"

"I don't have the time, Gervase," she said. "I'm out a lot."

Magritte and Dali, drawn to play Chaplin and O'Neill today for the right to play the winner of the Chekhov–Miller versus Cocteau–Picasso match, upped their offer of the previous round and proposed that they play Chaplin, O'Neill, Chekhov, Miller, Cocteau and Picasso in a "fabulous once-only premier spectacular event," to save time.

"No," said Darwin, uncertain how this would evolve. "What would we do if you lost? We would have six winners of one match."

"If you accept our proposal," said Dali, "we will undertake not to lose."

"Thank you," said Darwin, not wishing to create a precedent. "We'll let you know."

Their offer rejected, Magritte and Dali won two games in the first set against Chaplin and O'Neill and sat down to discuss progress. They identified two problems. O'Neill was solid, strong and had the endurance of a Clydesdale. Chaplin was confident, quick and clever like a fox.

Magritte and Dali decided to have their racquets restrung very loosely. When play started again, they found that if they didn't "middle the ball" they could bend it in unusual ways and vary its pace alarmingly. Chaplin and O'Neill protested that string tensions should be standardized and Dali offered to "doctor" their strings. The Americans decided on a policy of hitting winners but, with the ball describing extraordinary parabolas, and their opponents among the quickest in the competition, this approach was not without its problems. Chaplin's speed and O'Neill's slowness were increasingly manipulated to heighten the peculiar sensation that everything was happening in a new type of gravity. In the end the Americans couldn't get off court fast enough.

Day 35

Akhmatova v. Arendt • Magritte and Dali v. Chekhov and Miller • Chandler and Hammett v. Beckett and Duchamp • Lenya and Dietrich v. Sackville-West and Stephen-Woolf • Mansfield and Hodgkins v. Keller and Sullivan • Lawrence and Mansfield v. Bankhead and partner • Astaire and Rogers v. Freud and Klein

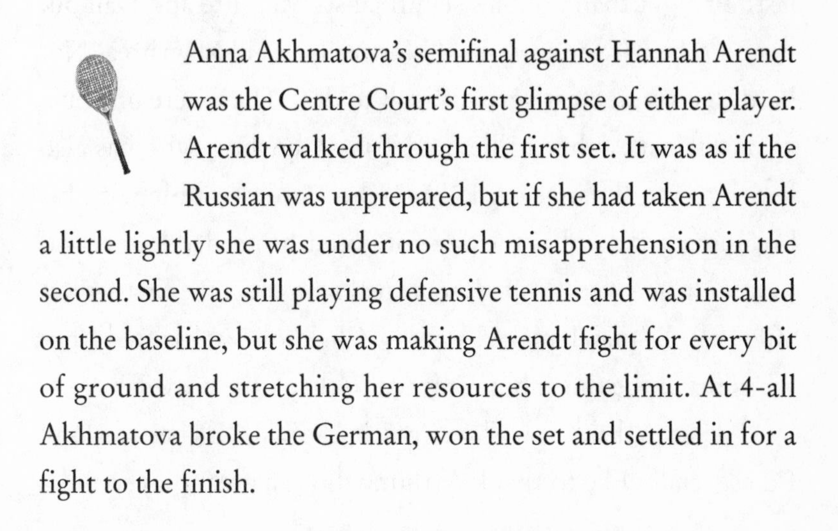

Anna Akhmatova's semifinal against Hannah Arendt was the Centre Court's first glimpse of either player. Arendt walked through the first set. It was as if the Russian was unprepared, but if she had taken Arendt a little lightly she was under no such misapprehension in the second. She was still playing defensive tennis and was installed on the baseline, but she was making Arendt fight for every bit of ground and stretching her resources to the limit. At 4-all Akhmatova broke the German, won the set and settled in for a fight to the finish.

Arendt came out playing like a winner. At the other end, Akhmatova kept her nerve and waited for her opportunity. It came at 5–5. Arendt took a bit off her serve and Akhmatova hit three low returns at her feet. Arendt got it back to 30–40 with two scorching serves but it was still break point.

The next serve was even faster and wide to the forehand, taking Akhmatova out of court. She got to it and pushed a return back, almost over the umpire's chair. Arendt waited and smashed. Akhmatova was there and somehow drove it deep into the ad court. The Arendt backhand was level to the task but it found the Russian at the net like a wolf. This was the moment that swung the match. Arendt came back and put enormous pressure on the Akhmatova service but, even though it went to deuce three times, it held for the match.

There might be someone who has played more tennis in the last fortnight than doubles semifinalists Magritte and Dali but it would be hard to imagine. "Not really," said Magritte. "Not hard to imagine. Just very difficult to do." They were on court again against Arthur Miller and Tony Chekhov, who has also had a very full dance card. Today he was in trouble with his breathing early and as the day got hotter he needed longer and longer changeovers. Miller's serve had won them the first set but after that the match played as it lay. Chekhov was assisted from the court at the finish but returned to thank the crowd.

"I'd like to thank you all very much," he said. "It's been realism. I'd especially like to thank Arthur, who is a great player and a good friend. Now, if it's all the same with you, I'd like to go to Moscow."

The Chandler and Hammett versus Beckett and Duchamp semi was another thing altogether. The Americans had spent the previous evening with Edna St. Vincent Millay and looked a little tired. Millay was in the stand looking relaxed. Beckett and Duchamp had spent all night in "some café somewhere on the Black Bush," so honors were even at the start and the first set had a haphazard quality. Shots were sprayed everywhere. The Americans took it when the Hammett serve started to fire, a process he described: "Like shelling peas. Big peas. And shelling them real fast. Wait a minute. Maybe not peas. Bigger than peas. Pumpkins maybe. It was like shelling pumpkins."

"Avocados," said Chandler.

"What?"

"Avocados."

"Some Californian crap is that, Ray?"

"I was thinking of something more the size of a tennis ball."

"Well, don't."

"Sorry."

"No one shells avocados," said Hammett.

"Pretend I never spoke," said Chandler.

"An avocado doesn't have a goddam shell."

"Nobody home at the Chandler house. Please call back later."

Beckett and Duchamp got going in the second set, taking it and the third. The fourth could have gone either way but, almost as if they had arranged it, they broke Hammett in the eighth game.

"I sat there with Hammett in the break at 4–5 in the fourth," said Chandler. "He tried to talk. I stopped him. It'd keep. The guys up the other end didn't believe our story anyway. Edna looked great but otherwise this boat was going nowhere. I stared at my racquet. You'd think they'd be able to come up with one of these that actually works. There were people dressed in mattresses floating about putting space stations together in slow motion on the news. And I was sitting there with technology I couldn't even drink."

The Americans left to a rousing reception. "We'll be back," they said, "when the movie comes out."

Lenya and Dietrich played gallantly in the first women's doubles semi, working the room well. When Sackville-West and Stephen-Woolf disputed a line call at 3–3 in the first set, they lost the support of the crowd. Dietrich was going to play in the final come hell or high water. Her serving in the final set was supreme, and she and Lenya played the big points better.

Mansfield and Hodgkins beat Keller and Sullivan for a berth in the final. Mansfield is the one to watch here. She seems to be doing so little, but what she does is so good. She is not a great spoiler and no power player. She gets in a side door and makes off through the window like a kid with a cake. Her health is a concern, however, and the effort proved taxing. A short while later she was on court again in the mixed but it was a huge ask and the weaker she got the more Lawrence of Nottingham berated her. "I like my women strong," he said. "What is the matter with you?"

"I'm not a hundred percent fit," said Mansfield. "That's what's the matter. Thanks for your sympathy."

"You should be like a train. Driving. Onward. We're not going to win like this. Where is your thrust?"

"Perhaps if you got your serve in and stopped being quite so repulsive, we might get out of this."

It was not to be. Lawrence said later that he had done what he could for women but there was "no helping some of them."

The other semi in the mixed was a real upset. Astaire and Rogers didn't want the win as badly as Freud and Klein. The Austrians concentrated on Rogers in the first set, whom Freud thought "a hysteric," and on Astaire in the second, whom Klein thought "very charming indeed."

Finals

Day 36

Freud and Klein v. Bankhead and partner • Lenya and Dietrich v. Mansfield and Hodgkins • Magritte and Dali v. Beckett and Duchamp • Millay v. Akhmatova • Joyce v. Orwell

Today eighteen billion viewers in 512 countries tuned in to the live broadcast of the finals.

"This figure is staggering," said George Plimpton. "Everyone knew there'd be an audience for this thing but what we're looking at here is the highest rating for a single event in sporting history."

"Not just in *sporting* history," added Norman Mailer. "This is an audience far beyond that of any previous *television* event. Far beyond."

It is certainly an audience well north of the wildest dreams

of the WTO. Nike's Friedrich Nietzsche confirmed that sponsors "are now looking at a minimum of fifteen to twenty million dollars per player for an annual contract. Take Picasso—he was knocked out of the singles in the second round but he's apparently negotiating a lifetime deal worth an estimated $400 million."

Many players have rejected the blandishments of management and the corporates but, for those who want it, fortunes are there for the taking. Keynes, Chaplin, Hemingway, Mae West, Bill Fields, Wodehouse, Sartre and de Beauvoir, Chanel, Sackville-West, Frankie Wright, Crosby and Disney have all become millionaires.

On the other hand, men's singles finalists Orwell and Joyce have constant money worries and have only been able to compete here through the assistance of friends. Van Gogh has to give lessons to kids in Arles to buy bread. "There's a lot of money about," said Nietzsche, "but it's not well distributed. Anyway, in terms of the individual, the money isn't the point. The title is the thing."

Roland Barthes "wasn't surprised" by the huge popularity of the event, elaborating that it "depended on what you mean by 'the event.' The original event has been colonized by its own discourse. Discourse is now the event."

Oscar Wilde mourned the tournament's popularity as "a requiem for genius. We stand on the threshold of idiocy and the army of commerce is advancing.

"All men kill the thing they love
In deciding to be bought.

Some do it very early
And some as a last resort.
The coward does it through endorsements
The brave man, on the court."

Were there other trends which worried him?

"All trends give rise to the gravest possible concern," Wilde said. "A trend is a lack of imagination masquerading as an idea. It has neither the appeal of the former, nor the rigor of the latter. There was a trend to fidelity in marriage at one point. It almost completely destroyed conversation."

Was he concerned about the trend to nationalism?

"An excellent example. Either these flags go, or I do."

As the mixed-doubles final got under way it was evident that Freud and Klein had done some homework on Bankhead and were playing to a plan. What was less obvious was that Bankhead had done some homework on Freud and Klein and was playing to another plan altogether.

When Bankhead and her partner took the first set, Freud said he regarded this as aggressive behavior.

"Really?" said Bankhead. "I thought we were rather demure."

"You think we are your parents," announced the Doc, "and we are engaged in the primal scene. This enrages you and you want to kill us."

"You are my parents?" checked Bankhead. "And what is it that enrages me so?"

"We are engaged in the primal scene."

"Goodness, how interesting. And what is that?"

"The act of sexual congress. Children have in their heads an image of their parents in congress. Do you know Plato's theory of forms?"

"I spent an evening with Chico Marx once. We spoke of little else."

"Plato's idea of 'form' is that certain ideas, or 'forms,' exist in our minds, and that if they did not we wouldn't recognize objects in the real world."

"Has anyone ever told you you're very attractive?" crooned Bankhead.

"Very interesting," said the Doc. "In what way?"

"Not you," said Bankhead. "You, Melanie."

Freud was grim when play resumed. He stood at the net like a customs official, jumping on anything he could reach and confiscating it. He glowered and he focused, and every time he drifted toward the center Bankhead and her partner put the ball past him down the line. Freud then decided he should be behind Klein and they changed places. He couldn't stay out of the action, though, and every time he strayed toward the net Bankhead and her partner put the ball behind him. The matter was wrapped up in two sets, the players waved to the crowd and left the arena. Bankhead refused to say who her partner was but said she'd be thanking him later. She said she had enjoyed the match, "Except for that little man who wanted to talk about sex. Good grief. I'm only playing tennis for a rest."

The mixed-doubles final had been an anticlimax and the organizers were anxious. Freud, one of the great authorities on doubles play, had just blown a great opportunity and the identity of one of the winners remained a mystery. (It was apparently not Douglas Fairbanks Jr.) In addition, the women's doubles final was a marketer's nightmare. It featured the twelfth seeds, who were two little-known New Zealanders, one of whom struggles with injury and has changed hotels four times. Like many players, Katherine Mansfield suffers from respiratory complaints and is vulnerable to changes in the weather.

When the players emerged, the professionals Lenya and Dietrich went about their preparations with Teutonic efficiency. Mansfield and Hodgkins appeared bewildered and had, in any case, very little to prepare. Each had one racquet and each hung a cardigan over the back of a chair before wandering onto the court. Dietrich was on song early and Lenya can hold her own in any company. Mansfield sat slumped during the breaks, coughing. It didn't look good.

The Europeans raced through the first set and it was 3–3 in the second before there was any indication this wasn't going to be a cakewalk. With Hodgkins playing superbly at the net, the Kiwis broke Dietrich and hung on. Dietrich left the court and changed her dress for the next set, returning in a figure-hugging wet-look creation which did a great deal for Internet service providers.

The third set was agonizing and exhilarating. Mansfield grew weaker and weaker but was the key player. Enchanted by her wounded brilliance, the French crowd embraced her, encouraged her, and lifted her. At 2–2 she hit three of the best returns in the match and the antipodeans went a break up. At 4–2 she netted two regulation overheads and lost her own serve. At 5–4, by which time she could hardly move, Mansfield came up with a forehand drive that ripped past Lenya like a bullet, then a perfectly judged drop shot. The crowd was ecstatic. People were standing, applauding wildly, with tears streaming down their faces. This was heroic stuff.

It was now match point.

Dietrich got the serve back but without much on it, Hodgkins across court. Lenya the drive. Mansfield looked out of position but she got to the ball and hit a crosscourt forehand which was a winner from the moment it left the racquet. The crowd went bananas. Hodgkins hoisted Mansfield in the air. At the press conference, though, Hodgkins was alone. "Katherine isn't well," she said.

"Where is she?" asked Mailer.

"She is in hospital," said Hodgkins.

"Will she be OK?"

"We don't know. Whatever happens, today Katherine was perfect. She had a great time here. She got to see Chekhov. She is very happy."

Magritte and Dali, back on Centre Court for the men's doubles final, entertained from the outset. Noticing the large video display which had been installed at the northern end for spectators without tickets, Dali spent the first set getting to the ball early, grinning at the cameras, saying, "Ladies and Gentlemen: the

Great Dali!," before playing his shot. The quieter Magritte had an idea of his own. He kept the ball between his head and the camera at all times so that the image projected around the world was of a neatly dressed man, behaving perfectly normally, with a tennis ball instead of a face.

In the second set, the Great Dali was generating such topspin that the ball would loop high away over the backline before it drifted back to drop just inside the line. Duchamp got to grips with this late in the set but by then the damage was done. Dali and Magritte were in command and the crowd had come to accept that if something looked possible, it was possible.

In the third set Beckett became obsessed with using a different ball each time he served. He put one in the left-hand pocket of his shorts and another in the right-hand pocket of his shorts. He put one down his left sock and one down his right sock. He put one up his left sleeve and another up his right sleeve. He held two in his right hand and two in his left hand. Beckett served using one of the balls in his left hand. He then moved the remaining ball into the "ready" position, shifted the uppermost ball from his right hand into his left hand, moved the ball from up his left shirtsleeve into his right hand, the ball from his right shirtsleeve into his left shirtsleeve and the ball from his right sock up into his right shirtsleeve. He then transferred the ball from his left sock into his right sock and shifted the one from his right shorts pockets into his left sock and put the one from his left shorts pocket into his right shorts pocket. Then, calling for an extra ball, he sequestered it accordingly, in the left shorts pocket vacated by this last action. He served again, using the next ball, replacing it with the ball below it and shifting one of the balls in his right hand into his left hand. He then . . .

Duchamp stepped in. "See that stand the umpire's sitting in?"

"I do," said Beckett.

"It's a bride descending a staircase as viewed through a small hole in a fence."

"Of course it is," said Beckett.

"Serve low to Dali's forehand and don't follow it in."

Beckett followed the instructions. As the serve passed Duchamp, he moved to cover the return down the line. Dali lifted the ball across court and Beckett drove it back between them. This was bread and butter for Beckett. One break won them the set. They repeated the pattern in the next and the match went to a fifth. There was no longer any display from Dali and Magritte. No Great Dali, no man with a ball for a face.

Duchamp and Beckett were now in a familiar position. One set remaining, all other complications out of the way, someone would move, someone would counter, another move, another counter, the games running out all the time. And so it was. Games went with service until 8–8, Dali serving. He hit a superb cross-court drive at 30-all. Duchamp got to it and threw it high to the backcourt. Magritte smashed, Beckett got it back, Dali went for the winner but hit it long. 30–40. Good serve, deep to the backhand. Beckett whipped it back and came in after it. Dali went down the line, Duchamp got it back across court. Magritte lobbed and Beckett hit a backhand smash for a winner. That was the break and Beckett served out the match at 10–8. By the time the microphone and the carpet and trophies were brought out, Beckett and Duchamp had slipped quietly away. Dali and Magritte were magnanimous in defeat. It had been a worthy final and tournament organizers were now relaxed and enjoying themselves enormously.

Anna Akhmatova was focused from the moment she came out for the women's final. Her presence was a testimony to endurance. After a promising career as a junior, she seemed headed for the Russian national squad but was taken to task by her coaches for her playing style. She silenced her critics when she won the Russian Open but, in the weeks following, her husband was killed. After a break from the game she came back and again won the national title. She was then banned from playing altogether and her son and second husband were imprisoned. Once more she disappeared from the circuit.

All the time, however, she worked on her game; she studied the play of Chekhov and Pushkin, Blok, Pasternak and Mandelstam, and she maintained her fitness. She arrived in Paris as part of the national team but, as with many of her fellow players, she represented both a tribute and a threat to Russian tennis. Akhmatova had strong wins against Pearl Buck and Elizabeth Bowen, got past Josephine Baker and then bamboozled top Englishwoman Virginia Stephen-Woolf before knocking out number two seed Sarah Bernhardt. If anyone has earned a place in a final here it is Akhmatova.

Millay also had an interrupted preparation. Impressive wins in the first few rounds preceded penetration of the Stopes defense and an outflanking of the Pavlova attack. Her next match was canceled after the unexpected death of Bessie Smith and since that time Millay has not picked up a racquet. She has been out every night with friends and has been paying close attention to the men's doubles, which she describes as "very tiring."

She was nervous during the hit-up and twice returned to the locker room, but as the first set developed she became steady as a rock. Akhmatova also took several games to acclimatize and Millay, well supported by a group of attractive men in dressing gowns, broke the Russian's serve at 5–5 and took the first set 7–5. If Akhmatova wanted this match, she was going to have to win it.

In the second set Akhmatova hustled better and we began to see her hand on the tiller. She served deeper, forcing Millay back and making her returns more defensive. She volleyed more often, making Millay play a more responsive game, and she dictated terms at the net. Millay played some lovely drop shots from the baseline, which delighted the dressing gowns but it wasn't enough to save the second set.

Millay came out of the blocks well in the third and bolted to a 3–0 lead before the Russian got on the board. Looking as if the trials of Sisyphus were upon her, Akhmatova dragged herself about the court. She stemmed the bleeding by breaking Millay at 2–3 with three sizzling returns. Millay served two double faults to lose her serve at 7–7 and the match looked to swing the Russian's way, but Millay came back and at 10-all it was clear the broadcast would run over time. At 12-all Millay went ahead. Akhmatova broke back. At 14-all Ahkmatova broke, only to be gathered in the next game. At 17-all Akhmatova broke again.

A hush fell over the stadium. This had the whiff of destiny about it.

Akhmatova served. Millay got to it but pushed it wide. Akhmatova served. Millay hit a crosscourt winner. Akhmatova served. Millay backhand lofted long. Akhmatova served. Ace. Match point. Akhmatova served, Millay good return, Akhmatova down the line, Millay crosscourt, Akhmatova deep to the forehand, Millay lob, Akhmatova smash. Millay got to it but couldn't control it; the ball drifted out. The Russian was the champion.

For someone who had just endured the trials of Job, Akhmatova had a very light touch. She thanked the crowd, said Millay had played brilliantly and that this was "a match without a hero." "We don't know what we're capable of until we are tested," she said. "As a general rule we are not being tested when we are being told we are being tested. We are being tested to the limit of human endurance when we are being told everything is normal. I'd like to dedicate this win to Osip Mandelstam, who is dead, and to Nadezhda, who is alive."

The men's finalists, fifth-seeded continental Dubliner James Joyce and the unseeded Englishman George Orwell, were given a standing ovation before the match had even started. Neither man is much accustomed to success and their attempt to acknowledge the spectators and behave like stars was endearing. They stood at the net, bowed slightly and pretended to be interested in their racquet strings. Orwell did up his shoes three times. Joyce fiddled with his glasses as if he'd never seen them before. They were both relieved to get on the court, hit the ball and lose themselves in their work.

To get here Orwell looked the facts in the face and dealt with them. He got past Harry Arlen, Ford Madox Ford and Louis Armstrong. He beat Eddie Munch in three and outlasted the astonishing van Gogh before defeating Fats Waller and Duchamp to reach the final.

In the top half of the draw, meanwhile, Joyce had invented a new way of playing and had beaten allcomers: his friend Bartók, Kipling the old warhorse, the powerful Rachmaninov, the energetic Spockster and the Great Dali. He then conquered his own hero Chekhov and, semifinally, in the match promoted on television as "the irresistible force versus the immovable object," he threw a net over SuperTom.

Orwell first grabbed the initiative in this match. A great reader of his opponent, he attacked as if he knew Joyce would reach his cruising height around game ten or twelve, playing long rhythmic points and dictating the form and structure of the match. Orwell intended to get on the board before that happened. If he left it too late the task might well be insurmountable. The Englishman got in and thumped the ball early, short, flat, fast, across court, forcing Joyce to scramble and not allowing any rhythm to develop. It wasn't pretty and it wasn't what a lot of the crowd had come to see, but Orwell wasn't an artist painting a picture; he was an engineer diverting a river.

It worked. Orwell had a set in the bag.

When Joyce did respond, midway through the second, he turned on a display of unforgettable tennis. He wasn't Orwell and he wasn't going to play like Orwell. He was Joyce. He would play like Joyce, and if he could play like Joyce at the top of his form he would be playing like no one else before or since.

He started hitting the ball deeper, taking control. All Orwell could do, forced further back, was defend, improvise and hope. The Irishman was not only seeing it well now but was lost in the sound—the sound of the play, of the crowd of onlookenpeepers and of his own voice, a muttering, dancing singsong of words and noises and thoughts and ideas and commentary. This is what he had done against SuperTom. It was like a tide of tennis rather than a match.

Joyce won the second set and swept through the third. He broke Orwell at 2–2 in the fourth and held the break. At 5–4 he was serving for the match.

With nothing left to lose, Orwell hit two beautiful crosscourt returns and a viciously sliced drop shot to get a break point. He then won the game with a simple lob—it wasn't deep, it had no spin. It was like a shot played by a child. He repeated the same play in Joyce's next service game, this time with three forehand returns to Joyce's feet, taking the match to a fifth set.

Orwell sat for a long time in his chair before coming back out on court. He knew Joyce's odyssey would continue unabated. Orwell needed to find another way home. "I didn't have to play better tennis," Orwell said later. "I was never going to play better tennis than Jim. The second and third sets proved that. What I had to do was play better points." In the fifth set he concentrated only on the important points. He identified them carefully and he played them like a demon.

For Joyce it must have been like hearing a beautiful piece of music, and every now and then having to stop and wait while a number of wildebeest were removed from the auditorium. Long, richly detailed passages of play would suddenly find themselves shuddering to a halt while the doors were opened and Orwell's animals were herded outside.

At 4–4 Orwell decided it was now or never. He crept forward and put the Joyce second serve away three successive times. He lost the next two points but crowded the serve again and belted the passing shot to secure the break. The end came soon after.

The players thanked their supporters; this was unusual for Joyce. "I take my hat off to them," he said. "And I hope they'll be standing a few jars at O'Dwyers tonight. I'd like to thank that woman in bare feet over there—she knows why. We had a fine match, didn't we, George? Ah yes, a bit of exercise and a fine thing too. Great play today, George. Here's to you, man."

Orwell spoke briefly and with some difficulty before leaving "for tests."

"Thank you," he said. "It is a great thing to be up here with James Joyce. I'd like to suggest that when the heroes and highlights of this tournament are recalled, attention also be given to remembering the monsters, the failures, the infamy and the disgrace . . ." Orwell struggled to continue, but was assisted from the court. His words, painfully expressed yet defiant and clear, provided a somber conclusion. There was some unease in the stadium as his wife, Sonia, collected his belongings, thanked the crowd and left.

Sports historians may be interested to know that Orwell's possessions consisted of the men's singles trophy, a piece of paper inscribed with his children's story and a six-month-old slip from Ladbrokes, backing the following for a win:

Mixed doubles: Tallulah Bankhead and whoever.
Men's doubles: Beckett and Duchamp.
Women's doubles: Mansfield and Hodgkins.
Women's singles: Akhmatova.
Men's singles: Winston.

Results

MEN'S SINGLES

QUALIFYING ROUND

H. Green (Eng) d. R. Firbank (Eng) 6–4, 7–6, 2–6, 6–4
J. Masefield (Eng) d. T. M. Rattigan (Eng) 4–6, 3–6, 7–6, 7–6, 10–8
J. Hasek (Czech) d. C. Day-Lewis (Ire) 7–6, 7–6, 7–6
A. Ribeiro (Por) d. H. Crane (USA) 2–6, 6–3, 2–6, 6–3, 6–1
R. P. Warren (USA) d. A. Blok (Rus) 6–1, 4–6, 6–4, 6–4
A. Hitchcock (Eng) d. J. Cheever (USA) 6–4, 7–6, 3–6, 6–2
J. E. Rodo (Urg) d. L. Durrell (Eng) 6–4, 3–6, 6–2, 6–0
J. E. Rivera (Col) d. A. Burgess (Eng) 6–3, 6–3, 6–7, 6–7, 7–6
J. Berryman (USA) d. F. Capra (USA) 7–6, 7–6, 6–4
P. Eluard (Fra) d. A. Powell (Eng) 3–6, 2–6, 6–3, 6–0, 6–2
H. Villa-Lobos (Bra) d. R. M. Helpmann (Aust) 7–5, 5–7, 7–5, 5–7, 10–8
N. Kazantzakis (Gre) d. G. Greene (Eng) 2–6, 6–3, 6–3, 7–5
E. Lubitsch (Ger) d. I. B. Singer (Pol) 6–4, 6–7, 7–5, 2–6, 6–2
B. Spock (USA) d. J. R. R. Tolkien (S. Afr) 6–4, 0–6, 6–3, 6–2
S. Lewis (USA) d. H. MacDiarmid (Scot) 1–6, 6–2, 4–6, 7–6, 6–3
A. A. Milne (Eng) d. P. E. Borduas (Can) 7–5, 6–4, 3–6, 6–1
J. B. Morton (Nark and Eng) d. M. Beckmann (Ger) 6–3, 6–4, 3–6, 6–2
S. Romberg (Hun) d. W. R. Reich (Ukr) 0–6, 6–3, 6–2, 6–0
J. Prevert (Fra) d. A. B. Paterson (Aust) 6–4, 6–7, 7–5, 6–3
E. Muir (Scot) d. N. Lindsay (Aust) 6–4, 6–3, 6–3
J. Galsworthy (Eng) d. J. S. Sargent (Eng) 3–6, 7–5, 7–5, 6–3
G. P. A. Grainger (Aust) d. F. R. Leavis (Eng) 6–1, 6–0, 6–4

ROUND ONE

(1)A. Chekhov (Rus) d. G. Mahler (Aut) 6–2, 6–7, 6–1, 6–3
(Q)G. P. A. Grainger (Aust) d. (Q)S. Romberg (Hun) 7–6, 6–7, 0–6, 7–6, 6–2
(Q)E. Muir (Scot) d. (Q)J. Galsworthy (Eng) 3–6, 6–7, 7–6, 6–4, 6–3
H. Toulouse-Lautrec (Fra) d. A. József (Hun) 7–6, 6–2, 4–6, 6–4
M. Chagall (URS) d. A. J. L. Cary (Ire) 3–6, 7–6, 7–5, 6–4
P. G. Wodehouse (Eng) d. A. N. Scriabin (Rus) 1–6, 7–6, 6–3, 6–7, 6–4
H. G. Wells (Eng) d. J. E. Vuillard (Fra) 6–3, 4–6, 6–3, 6–2
L. Hearn (USA) d. I. Grunewald (Swed) 7–6, 6–7, 6–4, 6–4
H. Matisse (Fra) d. A. Miller (USA) 2–6, 7–6, 6–7, 7–6, 6–4
D. Low (NZ) d. N. Rockwell (USA) 4–6, 6–2, 6–4, 7–5
S. B. Leacock (Can) d. (Q)H. Villa-Lobos (Bra) 7–6, 6–3, 6–2

F. Kreisler (Aut) d. P. Bonnard (Fra) 7–6, 7–6, 6–2
R. M. Rilke (Czech) d. R. L. Frost (USA) 3–6, 6–2, 7–6, 6–1
F. L. Wright (USA) d. (Q)J. Masefield (Eng) 6–4, 6–3, 6–4
P. Casals (Sp) d. P. Mondrian (Hol) 6–4, 5–7, 6–3, 6–4
(13)S. Freud (Aut) d. A. Gide (Fra) 3–6, 6–2, 2–6, 6–4, 6–1
(15)G. Puccini (Ita) d. D. D. Shostakovich (URS) 6–2, 3–6, 7–5, 6–2
E. Rutherford (NZ) d. S. Joplin (USA) 6–3, 3–6, 7–5, 5–7, 10–8
P. Klee (Switz) d. G. Roualt (Fra) 7–6, 7–6, 6–1
M. Proust (Fra) d. J. M. Synge (Ire) 6–1, 6–4, 6–7, 2–6, 11–9
W. C. Fields (USA) d. W. S. Maugham (Eng) 6–4, 4–6, 6–4, 4–6, 6–4
S. Dali (Sp) d. (Q)S. Lewis (USA) 4–6, 7–5, 4–6, 7–5, 11–9
H. Hesse (Ger) d. M. Ravel (Fra) 0–6, 6–4, 6–2, 6–1
C. S. Jung (Switz) d. F. I. Chaliapin (URS) 6–3, 6–7, 6–4, 6–4
S. P. Diaghilev (URS) d. A. E. John (Wa) 6–7, 6–4, 6–2, 6–2
(Q)B. Spock (USA) d. (Q)J. E. Rivero (Col) 6–4, 6–3, 7–5
B. Russell (Eng) d. R. Dufy (Fra) 6–4, 6–3, 7–5
J. Krishnamurti (Ind) d. F. Werfel (Aut) 7–5, 7–5, 6–3
S. Rachmaninov (URS) d. P. Valery (Fra) 3–6, 6–2, 6–1, 4–6, 11–9
H. L. Mencken (USA) d. M. Vlaminck (Fra) 6–2, 6–4, 6–3
J. R. Kipling (Eng) d. A. Schoenberg (Aut) 3–6, 6–4, 7–5, 6–4
(5)J. Joyce (Ire) d. B. Bartók (Hun) 6–4, 3–6, 7–6, 3–6, 14–12
(3)T. S. Eliot (USA) d. K. Capek (Czech) 6–4, 7–5, 6–2
H. L. Crosby (USA) d. N. P. Coward (Eng) 6–2, 6–1, 6–1
G. B. Shaw (Ire) d. L. Janáček (Czech) 3–6, 7–6, 7–6, 6–4
B. Keaton (USA) d. T. Tzara (Rom) 7–6, 4–6, 5–7, 6–2, 6–1
T. Hardy (Eng) d. A. Strindberg (Swed) 6–1, 1–6, 6–4, 6–4
A. Koestler (Hun) d. B. Brecht (Ger) 5–7, 6–2, 6–1, 6–4
R. Tagore (Ind) d. A. C. Debussy (Fra) 6–4, 5–7, 5–7, 7–5, 6–4
M. Gorky (Rus) d. A. Streeton (Aust) 6–2, 6–7, 6–4, 6–4
J. J. C. Sibelius (Fin) d. H. Gaudier-Brzeska (Fra) 7–5, 6–4, 6–2
(Q)J. Hasek (Czech) d. W. Gropius (Ger) 6–7, 7–5, 6–4, 7–5
D. H. Lawrence (Eng) d. A. Modigliani (Ita) 2–6, 7–5, 6–4, 6–2
L. Wittgenstein (Aut) d. W. C. Williams (USA) 1–6, 0–6, 7–5, 6–2, 6–2
D. Runyon (USA) d. F. Léger (Fra) 2–6, 2–6, 7–5, 6–1, 6–0
F. Kafka (Aut) d. G. D'Annunzio (Ita) 5–7, 6–4, 6–4, 6–3
J. M. Keynes (Eng) d. (Q)A. Ribeiro (Por) 4–6, 6–4, 1–6, 7–5, 6–2
(11)E. J. Paderewski (Pol) d. H. Bergson (Fra) 6–3, 6–4, 6–2

(9)B. Pasternak (Rus) d. J. Miró (Sp) 6–4, 6–3, 6–0
I. Stravinsky (URS) d. D. Rivera (Mex) 6–3, 6–2, 7–5
J. Cocteau (Fra) d. C. B. De Mille (USA) 6–4, 3–6, 7–6, 6–4
S. O'Casey (Ire) d. J. Epstein (Eng) 6–4, 6–3, 4–6, 7–5
R. C. Benchley (USA) d. E. Schiele (Aut) 4–6, 7–5, 6–2, 6–1
G. Apollinaire (Fra) d. T. Wilder (USA) 7–5, 6–4, 6–1
G. Moore (Ire) d. G. de Chirico (Hel) 2–6, 7–5, 6–3, 6–1
(Q)J. E. Rodo (Urg) d. R. Chandler (USA) 5–7, 5–7, 6–4, 7–5, 8–6
R. Carnap (Ger) d. M. Utrillo (Fra) 7–5, 6–4, 7–5
E. Satie (Fra) d. J. London (USA) 3–6, 6–4, 6–2, 6–7, 8–6
S. Eisenstein (URS) d. E. O'Neill (USA) 6–7, 7–6, 6–7, 7–6, 117–115
T. Mann (Ger) d. V. Kandinsky (URS) 0–6, 5–7, 6–4, 6–1, 6–3
C. Porter (USA) d. J. L. Borges (Arg) 6–4, 5–7, 6–3, 6–4
V. V. Mayakovsky (URS) d. H. Moore (Eng) 6–4, 6–1, 6–3
S. Prokofiev (URS) d. G Grosz (Ger) 7–6, 6–7, 1–0 (Grosz retired hurt.)
(8)L. Tolstoy (Rus) d. O. Kokoschka (Aut) 3–6, 6–3, 6–4, 6–4
(6)J. Conrad (Pol) d. R Graves (Ire) 6–2, 6–4, 6–2
W. C. Faulkner (USA) d. M. Ray (USA) 4–6, 2–6, 7–5, 7–5, 9–7
W. Benjamin (Ger) d. L. F. Celine (Fra) 6–0, 6–0, 6–0
J. Marx (USA) d. M. Heidegger (Ger) 0–6, 6–7, 6–3, 6–1, 6–0
A. Paton (S. Afr) d. R. Clair (Fra) 6–2, 6–2, 4–6, 6–4
K. Weill (Ger) d. A. Clarke (Ire) 5–7, 7–5, 7–5, 5–7, 9–7
P. Robeson (USA) d. O. Dix (Ger) 7–5, 7–5, 5–7, 7–5
A. Huxley (Eng) d. G. Simenon (Bel) 6–4, 6–4, 6–2
C. Pavese (Ita) d. F. Astaire (USA) 6–2, 6–4, 3–6, 1–6, 6–4
E. E. Cummings (USA) d. T. Wolfe (USA) 6–4, 3–6, 6–3, 5–7, 7–5
P. Neruda (Chile) d. F. S. Fitzgerald (USA) 6–7, 6–4, 6–3, 6–2
J. Renoir (Fra) d. V. Horowitz (URS) 6–4, 6–2, 7–5
V. S. Nabokov (URS) d. H. Miller (USA) 7–5, 6–4, 6–2
R. Lardner (USA) d. G. Miller (USA) 4–6, 6–4, 6–2, 6–4
H. Carmichael (USA) d. F. G. Lorca (Sp) 6–4, 4–6, 6–3, 5–7, 6–2
(14)C. Chaplin (Eng) d. C. E. Le Corbusier (Fra) 3–6, 7–5, 6–3, 5–7, 6–4
(10)M. Duchamp (Fra) d. (Q)A. A. Milne (Eng) 6–4, 6–4, 6–4
C. Isherwood (Eng) d. A. Breton (Fra) 1–6, 7–5, 2–6, 6–3, 6–0
J. P. Sartre (Fra) d. D. Ellington (USA) 2–6, 3–6, 7–6, 7–6, 7–6
O. Mandelstam (URS) d. C. Reed (Eng) 5–7, 6–3, 6–1, 6–1
L. Pirandello (Ita) d. E. M. Forster (Eng) 0–6, 6–4, 4–6, 6–4, 6–0

J. Lacan (Fra) d. J. Heifetz (URS) 3–6, 5–7, 6–4, 7–5, 6–3
E. Hemingway (USA) d. L. Visconti (Ita) 6–1, 7–5, 2–6, 6–4
K. Gödel (Aut) d. S. Spender (Eng) 7–5, 6–2, 6–2
C. Levi (Ita) d. L. Buñuel (Sp) 3–6, 6–2, 6–4, 6–4
L. MacNeice (Ire) d. A. Khatchaturian (URS) 7–5, 7–5, 5–7, 1–6, 6–4
E. Caruso (Ita) d. D. W. Griffith (USA) 7–6, 5–7, 7–5, 6–7, 7–5
A. Malraux (Fra) d. B. Beiderbecke (USA) 6–1, 5–7, 6–2, 6–2
E. Waugh (Eng) d. V. de Sica (Ita) 6–1, 6–3, 5–7, 6–4
J. Steinbeck (USA) d. A. P. Moravia (Ita) 6–4, 7–5, 6–0
J. Thurber (USA) d. (Q)H. Green (Eng) 7–5, 6–2, 6–4
(4)A. Einstein (Ger) d. J. H. Arp (Fra) 6–4, 6–3, 6–1
(7)P. Picasso (Sp) d. K. S. Stanislavsky (Rus) 6–2, 6–3, 6–7, 6–1
S. Beckett (Ire) d. E. Canetti (Bul) 0–6, 1–6, 6–3, 6–3, 6–3
E. Munch (Nor) d. D. Oistrakh (URS) 4–6, 7–5, 7–5, 6–3
J. Betjeman (Eng) d. F. Bacon (Ire) 6–2, 4–6, 7–5, 6–4
L. Armstrong (USA) d. M. Carne (Fra) 6–2, 6–1, 7–5
W. H. Auden (Eng) d. G. K. Chesterton (Eng) 2–6, 0–6, 7–6, 6–1, 6–4
G. Orwell (Eng) d. H. Arlen (USA) 6–3, 7–5, 6–2
F. M. Ford (USA) d. S. O'Faoláin (Ire) 4–6, 5–7, 7–5, 6–1, 6–2
B. Hecht (USA) d. (Q)J. Berryman (USA) 0–6, 5–7, 6–4, 6–4, 6–0
E. Nolde (Ger) d. F. Picabia (Fra) 6–4, 6–4, 2–6, 5–7, 6–4
(Q)N. Kazantzakis (Gre) d. H. H. Munro (Eng) 4–6, 6–2, 6–1, 6–4
R. Magritte (Bel)
A. Bierce (USA) d. L. Bakst (URS) 6–4, 6–3, 6–2
H. Rousseau (Fra) d. F. Delius (Eng) 7–6, 2–6, 3–6, 6–4, 6–4
W. de Kooning (Hol) d. J. Dos Passos (USA) 2–6, 6–2, 6–1, 6–4
(12)V. van Gogh (Hol) d. C. Cavafy (Hel) 4–6, 6–3, 6–2, 6–4
(16)V. Nijinsky (Pol) d. (Q)E. Lubitsch (Ger) 6–1, 6–0, 0–6, 6–2
L. P. Hartley (Eng) d. A. Copland (USA) 2–6, 6–4, 4–6, 6–2, 6–3
A. Schweitzer (Ger) d. A. Giacometti (Switz) 6–3, 6–4, 6–4
M. C. Escher (Hol) d. A. Beardsley (Eng) 6–2, 6–1, 6–0
G. Seurat (Fra) d. W. Sickert (Eng) 6–1, 6–1, 6–0
M. Ernst (Ger) d. (Q)R. P. Warren (USA) 7–5, 6–4, 6–4
S. Crane (USA) d. T. Dreiser (USA) 6–3, 6–3, 2–6, 6–4
T. Waller (USA) d. (Q)A. Hitchcock (Eng) 6–0, 6–0, 6–0
(Q)J. B. Morton (Nark and Eng) d. K. Gibran (Leb) 3–6, 6–4, 6–3, 6–1
G. L. Strachey (Eng) d. W. Disney (USA) 6–0, 6–1, 6–1

A. Segovia (Sp) d. R. Campbell (S. Afr) 6–4, 6–4, 6–4
G. Gershwin (USA) d. (Q)P. Eluard (Fra) 4–6, 6–2, 6–1, 6–4
(Q)J. Prevert (Fra) d. G. Autrey (USA) 6–4, 7–5, 5–7, 1–6, 8–6
A. Derain (Fra) d. A. Rubinstein (Pol) 6–4, 6–2, 6–4
E. Fermi (Ita) d. A. Toscanini (Ita) 4–6, 6–1, 6–1, 6–1
(2)W. B. Yeats (Ire) d. G. Klimt (Aut) 3–6, 7–6, 6–4, 6–4

ROUND TWO

(1)A. Chekhov (Rus) d. G. P. A. Grainger (Aust) 7–5, 6–2, 6–1
(Q)E. Muir (Scot) d. H. Toulouse-Lautrec (Fra) 4–6, 7–6, 6–2, 6–4
P. G. Wodehouse (Eng) d. M. Chagall (URS) 3–6, 5–7, 6–4, 6–3, 6–1
H. G. Wells (Eng) d. L. Hearn (Jap) and R. West (Ire) 6–3, 6–2, 1–6, 7–5
H. Matisse (Fra) d. D. Low (NZ) 6–3, 2–6, 7–5, 1–6, 14–12.
S. B. Leacock (Can) d. F. Kreisler (Aut) 4–6, 7–5, 6–4, 6–2
R. M. Rilke (Czech) d. F. L. Wright (USA) 6–3, 4–6, 7–6, 5–7, 6–2
(13)S. Freud (Aut) d. P. Casals (Sp) 6–2, 6–4, 6–4
(15)G. Puccini (Ita) d. E. Rutherford (NZ) 6–4, 5–7, 6–2, 6–4
M. Proust (Fra) d. P. Klee (Switz) 6–4, 7–5, 5–7, 6–1
S. Dali (Sp) d. W. C. Fields (USA) 6–3, 3–6, 2–6, 2–4 (Fields forfeited due to prolonged absence.)
C. S. Jung (Switz) d. H. Hesse (Ger) 4–6, 6–3, 6–4, 1–6, 7–5
(Q)B. Spock (USA) d. S. P. Diaghilev (URS) 6–2, 6–4, 7–5
B. Russell (Eng) d. J. Krishnamurti (Ind) 2–6, 6–4, 6–1, 6–4
S. Rachmaninov (URS) d. H. L. Mencken (USA) 3–6, 6–2, 6–4, 6–1
(5)J. Joyce (Ire) d. J. R. Kipling (Eng) 3–6, 7–5, 6–4, 6–2
(3)T. S. Eliot (USA) d. H. L. Crosby (USA) 6–2, 6–2, 6–0
G. B. Shaw (Ire) d. B. Keaton (USA) 6–3, 6–2, 7–6
T. Hardy (Eng) d. A. Koestler (Hun) 6–2, 6–4, 6–1
R. Tagore (Ind) d. M. Gorky (URS) 6–4, 6–2, 3–6, 7–6
(Q)J. Hasek (Czech) d. J. J. C. Sibelius (Fin) 6–4, 5–7, 6–3, 6–2
L. Wittgenstein (Aut) d. D. H. Lawrence (Eng) 6–2, 6–1, 6–1
F. Kafka (Czech) d. D. Runyon (USA) 2–6, 2–6, 6–3, 6–1, 6–3
J. M. Keynes (Eng) d. **(11)E. J. Paderewski (Pol)** 1–6, 5–7, 6–3, 6–4, 8–6
I. Stravinsky (URS) d. **(9)B. Pasternak (Rus)** 3–6, 6–7, 6–4, 6–2, 6–4
S. O'Casey (Ire) d. J. Cocteau (Fra) 6–2, 4–6, 6–7, 6–4, 6–4
R. C. Benchley (USA) d. G. Apollinaire (Fra) 1–6, 6–4, 7–5, 6–4
(Q)J. E. Rodo (Urg) d. G. Moore (Ire) 6–4, 6–3, 2–6, 7–5

E. Satie (Fra) d. R. Carnap (Ger) 3–6, 6–4, 6–2, 6–2
T. Mann (Ger) d. S. Eisenstein (URS) 4–6, 5–7, 7–5, 6–4, 6–4
V. V. Mayakovsky (URS) d. C. Porter (USA) 3–6, 6–4, 7–5, 0–3 (Porter forfeited due to injury.)
(8)L. Tolstoy (Rus) d. S. Prokofiev (URS) 7–5, 6–4, 2–6, 7–5
W. C. Faulkner (USA) d. **(6)J. Conrad (Pol)** 6–3, 5–7, 6–4, 6–2
J. Marx (USA) d. W. Benjamin (Ger) 2–6, 6–4, 6–1, 2–2 (Benjamin forfeited due to injury.)
A. Paton (S. Afr) d. K. Weill (Ger) 4–6, 6–2, 7–5, 6–4
P. Robeson (USA) d. A. Huxley (Eng) 6–4, 7–5, 6–2
E. E. Cummings (USA) d. C. Pavese (Ita) 6–2, 6–3, 5–7, 5–7, 8–6
J. Renoir (Fra) d. P. Neruda (Chile) 6–1, 7–5, 6–2
R. Lardner (USA) d. V. S. Nabokov (URS) 6–4, 6–1, 6–3
(14)C. Chaplin (Eng) d. H. Carmichael (USA) 6–3, 6–3, 6–3
(10)M. Duchamp (Fra) d. C. Isherwood (Eng) 7–5, 6–4, 6–3
O. Mandelstam (URS) d. J. P. Sartre (Fra) 6–4, 6–2, 6–0
L. Pirandello (Ita) d. J. Lacan (Fra) 6–3, 6–4, 5–7, 6–3
E. Hemingway (USA) d. K. Gödel (Aut) 1–6, 0–6, 7–5, 7–5, 9–7
L. MacNeice (Ire) d. C. Levi (Ita) 2–6, 7–5, 6–4, 3–6, 6–3
A. Malraux (Fra) d. E. Caruso (Ita) 4–6, 6–2, 6–3, 6–2
J. Steinbeck (USA) d. E. Waugh (Eng) 1–6, 3–6, 7–5, 6–1, 6–0
(4)A. Einstein (Ger) d. J. Thurber (USA) 6–0, 4–6, 0–6, 6–4, 8–6
S. Beckett (Ire) d. **(7)P. Picasso (Sp)** 2–6, 4–6, 7–5, 6–0, 6–3
E. Munch (Nor) d. J. Betjeman (Eng) 6–3, 6–4, 5–7, 6–4
L. Armstrong (USA) d. W. H. Auden (Eng) 4–6, 2–6, 7–5, 6–4, 6–4
G. Orwell (Eng) d. F. M. Ford (Eng) 7–5, 6–3, 6–2
B. Hecht (USA) d. E. Nolde (Ger) 7–5, 6–3, 6–1
R. Magritte (Bel) d. (Q)N. Kazantzakis (Gre) 6–3, 7–5, 2–6, 6–4
A. Bierce (USA) d. H. Rousseau (Fra) 2–6, 7–5, 7–5, 7–5
(12)V. van Gogh (Hol) d. W. de Kooning (Hol) 4–6, 3–6, 6–0, 6–0, 6–0
(16)V. Nijinsky (URS) d. L. P. Hartley (Eng) 6–2, 6–1, 6–3
M. C. Escher (Hol) d. A. Schweitzer (Ger) 6–3, 6–4, 6–3
G. Seurat (Fra) d. M. Ernst (Ger) 3–6, 6–4, 5–7, 6–2, 9–7
T. Waller (USA) d. S. Crane (USA) 2–6, 6–4, 7–5, 6–1
(Q)J. B. Morton (Nark and Eng) d. G. L. Strachey (Eng) 7–5, 5–7, 6–4, 6–2
G. Gershwin (USA) d. A. Segovia (Sp) 4–6, 2–6, 7–5, 6–4, 6–4
A. Derain (Fra) d. (Q)J. Prevert (Fra) 6–3, 6–2, 6–3

(2)W. B. Yeats (Ire) d. E. Fermi (Ita) 6–4, 5–7, 6–4, 7–5

ROUND THREE

(1)A. Chekhov (Rus) d. (Q)E. Muir (Scot) 6–3, 7–6, 6–1
P. G. Wodehouse (Eng) d. H. G. Wells (Eng) 2–6, 6–3, 6–1, 6–2
H. Matisse (Fra) d. S. B. Leacock (Can) 6–4, 6–3, 1–6, 7–5
(13)S. Freud (Aut) d. R. M. Rilke (Czech) 6–3, 1–6, 0–6, 7–5, 9–7
M. Proust (Fra) d. **(15)G. Puccini (Ita)** 6–4, 6–3, 7–5
S. Dali (Sp) d. C. S. Jung (Switz) 6–1, 7–5, 6–7, 6–3
(Q)B. Spock (USA) d. B. Russell (Eng) 0–6, 6–4, 6–0, 6–0
(5)J. Joyce (Ire) d. S. Rachmaninov (URS) 6–4, 6–2, 4–6, 7–5
(3)T. S. Eliot (USA) d. G. B. Shaw (Ire) 4–6, 5–7, 6–4, 6–3, 7–5
R. Tagore (Ind) d. T. Hardy (Eng) 6–4, 7–5, 6–3
L. Wittgenstein (Aut) d. (Q)J. Hasek (Czech) 7–5, 7–5, 0–6, 6–4
F. Kafka (Czech) d. J. M. Keynes (Eng) 6–0, 6–0, (6–7*), 4–6, 6–4
I. Stravinsky (URS) d. S. O'Casey (Ire) 3–6, 6–4, 7–6 (8–6), 6–4
(Q)J. E. Rodo (Urg) d. R. C. Benchley (USA) 6–3, 2–6, 5–7, 7–5, 6–4
T. Mann (Ger) d. E. Satie (Fra) 6–3, 2–6, 6–3, 7–6
V. V. Mayakovsky (URS) d. **(8)L. Tolstoy (Rus)** 3–6, 7–6, 6–4, 6–2
W. C. Faulkner (USA) d. J. Marx (USA) 7–5, 6–2, 2–6, 4–6, 9–7
P. Robeson (USA) d. A. Paton (S. Afr) 6–4, 7–5, 6–2
E. E. Cummings (USA) d. J. Renoir (Fra) 6–4, 7–5, 7–5
R. Lardner (USA) d. **(14)C. Chaplin (Eng)** 4–6, 6–3, 6–4, 6–2
(10)M. Duchamp (Fra) d. O. Mandelstam (URS) 7–5, 6–7, 6–4, 7–5
E. Hemingway (USA) d. L. Pirandello (Ita) 6–4, 5–7, 2–6, 7–6, 6–4
A. Malraux (Fra) d. L. MacNeice (Ire) 7–5, 6–2, 6–4
(4)A. Einstein (Ger) d. J. Steinbeck (USA) 6–2, 6–4, 6–2
E. Munch (Nor) d. S. Beckett (Ire) 6–7, 7–5, 6–4, 14–12
G. Orwell (Eng) d. L. Armstrong (USA) 4–6, 6–2, 3–6, 7–5, 6–1
R. Magritte (Bel) d. B. Hecht (USA) 6–3, 6–2, 7–5
(12)V. van Gogh (Hol) d. A. Bierce (USA) 1–6, 3–6, 6–2, 6–1, 6–4
M. C. Escher (Hol) d. **(16)V. Nijinsky (URS)** 6–1, 1–6, 6–1, 1–6, 6–1
T. Waller (USA) d. G. Seurat (Fra) 6–3, 7–6, 6–4
G. Gershwin (USA) d. (Q)J. B. Morton (Nark and Eng) 6–4, 7–5, 6–4
(2)W. B. Yeats (Ire) d. A. Derain (Fra) 7–5, 6–2, 0–6, 2–6, 6–1

ROUND FOUR

(1)A. Chekhov (Rus) d. P. G. Wodehouse (Eng) 6–1, 6–3, 6–4
H. Matisse (Fra) d. **(13)S. Freud (Aut)** 6–3, 6–4, 5–7, 6–3
S. Dali (Sp) d. M. Proust (Fra) 3–6, 7–5, 6–2, 6–3
(5)J. Joyce (Ire) d. (Q)B. Spock (USA) 7–6 (18–16), 6–4, 6–3
(3)T. S. Eliot (USA) d. R. Tagore (Ind) 4–6, 7–5, 1–6, 6–4, 9–7
L. Wittgenstein (Aut) d. F. Kafka (Czech) 3–6, 1–6, 6–4, 7–5, 14–12
I. Stravinsky (URS) d. (Q)J. E. Rodo (Urg) 6–4, 7–5, 6–3
T. Mann (Ger) d. V. V. Mayakovsky (URS) 7–5, 4–6, 7–5, 6–2
W. C. Faulkner (USA) d. P. Robeson (USA) 4–6, 2–6, 6–2, 6–1, 6–1
R. Lardner (USA) d. E. E. Cummings (USA) 6–4, 2–6, 7–6, 6–2
(10)M. Duchamp (Fra) d. E. Hemingway (USA) 7–5, 6–4, 6–2
(4)A. Einstein (Ger) d. A. Malraux (Fra) 5–7, 6–4, 6–3, 6–2
G. Orwell (Eng) d. E. Munch (Nor) 6–3, 6–4, 6–3
(12)V. van Gogh (Hol) d. R. Magritte (Bel) 6–4, 6–4, 6–0
T. Waller (USA) d. M. C. Escher (Hol) 6–2, 6–4, 6–4
(2)W. B. Yeats (Ire) d. G. Gershwin (USA) 6–3, 6–4, 6–2

ROUND FIVE

(1)A. Chekhov (Rus) d. H. Matisse (Fra) 6–1, 6–2, 3–6, 0–6, 7–5
(5)J. Joyce (Ire) d. S. Dali (Sp) 6–4, 5–7, 6–2, 6–3
(3)T. S. Eliot (USA) d. L. Wittgenstein (Aut) 6–4, 7–5, 2–6, 1–6, 9–7
T. Mann (Ger) d. I. Stravinsky (URS) 6–4, 6–1, 7–5
R. Lardner (USA) d. W. C. Faulkner (USA) 6–4, 6–2, 4–6, 6–3
(10)M. Duchamp (Fra) d. **(4)A. Einstein (Ger)** 1–6, 6–4, 7–5, 6–4
G. Orwell (Eng) d. **(12)V. van Gogh (Hol)** 2–6, 5–7, 6–1, 6–4, 6–3
T. Waller (USA) d. **(2)W. B. Yeats (Ire)** 3–6, 5–7, 7–5, 6–3, 6–2

QUARTERFINALS

(5)J. Joyce (Ire) d. **(1)A. Chekhov (Rus)** 2–6, 4–6, 6–4, 6–3, 6–3
(3)T. S. Eliot (USA) d. T. Mann (Ger) 6–4, 5–7, 3–6, 6–3, 6–2
(10)M. Duchamp (Fra) d. R. Lardner (USA) 4–6, 3–6, 7–6, 7–6, 6–2
G. Orwell (Eng) d. T. Waller (USA) 7–5, 3–6, 6–3, 6–4

SEMIFINALS

(5)J. Joyce (Ire) d. **(3)T. S. Eliot (USA)** 6–4, 3–6, 4–6, 6–2, 6–3
G. Orwell (Eng) d. **(10)M. Duchamp (Fra)** 7–5, 6–3, 4–6, 4–6, 6–1

FINAL

G. Orwell (Eng) d. **(5)J. Joyce (Ire)** 6–4, 3–6, 1–6, 7–5, 6–4

WOMEN'S SINGLES

ROUND ONE

(1)A. Earhart (USA) d. G. O'Keeffe (USA) 6–3, 6–2
R. Luxemburg (Pol) d. L. Riefenstahl (Ger) 2–6, 6–0, 6–1
M. West (USA) d. I. Dinesen (Den) 7–5, 2–6, 6–1
S. Naidu (Ind) d. L. Gish (USA) 6–3, 6–4
C. E. Stead (Aust) d. S. Weill (Fra) 6–3, 6–1
C. I. (R.) West (Ire) d. A. Nin (Fra) 6–4, 6–3
A. Noether (Ger) d. H. Rubenstein (Pol) 6–3, 8–6
(9)A. Christie (Eng) d. A. Oakley (USA) 6–2, 6–4
(13)M. Montessori (Ita) d. N. Marsh (NZ) 7–5, 6–1
C. G. Markievicz (Ire) d. P. Negri (Pol) 6–1, 4–6, 6–4
B. Smith (USA) d. H. Sh'arawi (Egy) 5–7, 7–5, 6–4
T. Bankhead (USA) d. Q. Song (Chi) 6–1, 4–6, 6–4
E. Roosevelt (USA) d. A. Lowell (Boston) 6–3, 6–0
M. Gonne-MacBride (Ire) d. A. Loos (USA) 6–1, 6–4
M. Elliott (USA) d. M. Rambert (Eng) 6–2, 6–4
K. A. Porter (USA) d. **(5)E. Pankhurst (Eng)** 7–5, 6–1
(16)M. Pickford (USA) d. E. Post (USA) 6–1, 6–0
G. Swanson (USA) d. N. de Valois (Ire) 6–4, 3–6, 6–3
J. Rhys (Dom) d. B. Hepworth (Eng) 2–6, 7–5, 6–1
K. S. Prichard (Aust) d. D. Ibarruri (Sp) 6–4, 6–4
M. McCarthy (USA) d. H. Doolittle (USA) 6–2, 6–4
L. Hellman (USA) d. J. Rankin (USA) 7–5, 6–3
M. Renaud (Fra) d. H. H. Richardson (Aust) 7–6, 3–6, 7–6
(6)G. Stein (USA) d. M. Hari (Hol) 3–6, 7–6, 6–0
(3)A. Pavlova (URS) d. M. M. Dietrich (Ger) 6–2, 5–7, 6–2
M. Klein (Aut) d. S. Thorndike (Eng) 6–4, 7–5
M. Graham (USA) d. M. I. Tsvetaeva (URS) 6–4, 3–3 (Tsvetaeva forfeited due to injury.)
A. Nazimova (URS) d. S. T. Warner (Eng) 7–5, 6–4
A. Rand (URS) d. B. Potter (Eng) 6–1, 6–0
E. St. V. Millay (USA) d. N. Astor (Eng) 6–3, 7–5
A. Besant (Eng) d. M. Mitchell (USA) 6–2, 6–4

(11)M. C. C. Stopes (Scot) d. M. Moore (USA) 6–3, 6–4
(4)S. Bernhardt (Fra) d. E. Blyton (Eng) 6–3, 6–4
L. B. Lenya (Aut) d. M. Song (Chi) 6–4, 6–2
D. Parker (USA) d. E. Sitwell (Eng) 7–5, 6–2
W. Cather (USA) d. G. Richier (Fra) 7–6, 6–2
M. Yourcenar (Bel) d. D. L. Sayers (Eng) 7–6, 6–4
F. Hodgkins (NZ) d. F. Stark (Eng) 4–6, 7–5, 6–3
V. Sackville-West (Eng) d. L. Fontanne (USA) 6–2, 5–7, 6–2
(12) D. N. Melba (Aust) d. C. B. Luce (USA) 7–5, 7–5
(7)A. V. Stephen-Woolf (Eng) d. E. Schiaparelli (Ita/USA) 6–1, 6–2
K. Mansfield (NZ) d. B. Holliday (USA) 6–4, 7–5
E. Bishop (USA) d. E. Arden (Can) 6–3, 6–3
C. Claudine (Fra) d. F. Kahlo (Mex) 7–5, 6–2
J. Baker (Fra) d. B. Lillie (Can) 6–4, 4–6, 6–4
N. S. Goncharova (URS) d. L. S. Stern (Lat) 7–5, 4–6, 6–3
E. Bowen (Ire) d. E. Wharton (USA) 7–5, 6–3
(15)A. A. G. Akhmatova (URS) d. P. S. Buck (USA) 6–4, 6–7, 7–5
H. Arendt (Ger) d. **(8)G. Garbo (Swe)** 7–5, 5–7, 7–5
S. W. Beach (USA) d. E. Ferber (USA) 7–6, 6–3
S. Lagerlöf (Swe) d. M. P. Campbell (Eng) 6–3, 0–6, 6–2
D. M. Bates (Aust) d. I. Compton-Burnett (Eng) 6–2, 6–4
K. Cornell (USA) d. B. Cartland (Eng) 6–2, 6–0
A. Kollontai (URS) d. V. V. L. Pandit (Ind) 6–4, 6–1
N. Y. Mandelstam (URS) d. U. Kulthum (Egy) 6–4, 5–7, 7–5
I. Duncan (USA) d. **(14)M. Mead (USA)** 6–4, 6–2
(10)C. G. Chanel (Fra) d. T. Bara (USA) 6–3, 6–3
D. Barnes (USA) d. L. Pons (USA) 6–2, 4–6, 6–4
A. Pauker (Rom) d. A. L. Strong (USA) 5–7, 7–5, 7–5
A. Myrdal (Swe) d. M. Sanger (USA) 7–6, 6–2
G. Mistral (Chile) d. F. Ichikawa (Jap) 0–6, 7–6, 7–5
R. Draper (USA) d. K. Kollwitz (Ger) 6–2, 6–4
F. Brice (USA) d. S. Undset (Nor) 6–3, 6–1
(2)S. de Beauvoir (Fra) d. M. Garden (Scot) 6–4, 6–3

ROUND TWO

R. Luxemburg (Pol) d. **(1)A Earhart (USA)** 7–5, 6–4
S. Naidu (Ind) d. M. West (USA) 7–5, 6–0
C. E. Stead (Aust) d. C. I . (R.) West (Ire) 2–6, 6–4, 6–2
A. Noether (Ger) d. **(9)A. Christie (Eng)** (forfeit) (Anyone knowing anything about the whereabouts of Ms. Christie should contact the police immediately.)
(13)M. Montessori (Ita) d. C. G. Markievicz (Ire) 6–2, 5–7, 6–4
B. Smith (USA) d. T. Bankhead (USA) 6–4, 3–6, 6–3
E. Roosevelt (USA) d. M. Gonne-MacBride (Ire) 7–5, 6–3
M. Elliott (USA) d. K. A. Porter (USA) 7–5, 6–2
G. Swanson (USA) d. **(16)M. Pickford (USA)** 6–3, 6–4
J. Rhys (Dom) d. K. S. Prichard (Aust) 7–6, 6–7, 9–7
M. McCarthy (USA) d. L. Hellman (USA) 6–1, 6–4
(6)G. Stein (USA) d. M. Renaud (Fra) 6–1, 6–4
(3)A. Pavlova (URS) d. M. Klein (Aut) 6–2, 6–4
M. Graham (USA) d. A. Nazimova (URS) 6–4, 6–4
E. St. V. Millay (USA) d. A. Rand (URS) 6–4, 7–5 (pending protest)
(11)M. C. C. Stopes (Scot) d. A. Besant (Eng) 6–3, 6–2
(4)S. Bernhardt (Fra) d. L. B. Lenya (Aut) 6–1, 6–2
D. Parker (USA) d. W. Cather (USA) 6–2, 1–6, 6–4
F. Hodgkins (NZ) d. M. Yourcenar (Bel) 5–7, 7–5, 6–4
V. Sackville-West (Eng) d. **(12)D. N. Melba (Aust)** 2–6, 6–4, 6–4
(7)A. V. Stephen-Woolf (Eng) d. K. Mansfield (NZ) 7–5, 5–7, 9–7
E. Bishop (USA) d. C. Claudine (Fra) 6–3, 6–2
J. Baker (Fra) d. N. S. Goncharova (URS) 6–2, 6–2
(15)A. A. G. Akhmatova (URS) d. E. Bowen (Ire) 6–3, 6–2
H. Arendt (Ger) d. S. W. Beach (USA) 6–3, 7–5
D. M. Bates (Aust) d. S. Lagerlöf (Swe) 7–5, 6–1
A. Kollontai (URS) d. K. Cornell (USA) 5–7, 6–3, 7–5
N. Y. Mandelstam (URS) d. I. Duncan (USA) 2–6, 6–4, 3–3 (Duncan forfeited due to injury.)
(10)C. G. Chanel (Fra) d. D. Barnes (USA) 1–6, 7–5, 6–4
A. Pauker (Rom) d. A. Myrdal (Swe) 6–3, 6–4
R. Draper (USA) d. G. Mistral (Chile) 6–3, 7–5
(2)S. de Beauvoir (Fra) d. F. Brice (USA) 6–1, 6–0

ROUND THREE

R. Luxemburg (Pol) d. S. Naidu (Ind) 6–4, 6–3
C. E. Stead (Aust) d. A. Noether (Ger) 7–5, 6–2
B. Smith (USA) d. **(13)M. Montessori (Ita)** 6–4, 1–6, 6–2
M. Elliott (USA) d. E. Roosevelt (USA) 6–3, 6–3
J. Rhys (Dom) d. G. Swanson (USA) 6–2, 6–3
(6)G. Stein (USA) d. M. McCarthy (USA) 1–6, 7–5, 6–4
(3)A. Pavlova (URS) d. M. Graham (USA) 6–3, 6–4
E. St. V. Millay (USA) d. **(11)M. C. C. Stopes (Scot)** 7–6, 6–4
(4)S. Bernhardt (Fra) d. D. Parker (USA) 5–7, 7–5, 7–5
F. Hodgkins (NZ) d. V. Sackville-West (Eng) 6–4, 6–3
(7)A. V. Stephen-Woolf (Eng) d. E. Bishop (USA) 6–1, 3–6, 8–6
(15)A. A. G. Akhmatova (URS) d. J. Baker (Fra) 2–6, 6–4, 6–3
H. Arendt (Ger) d. D. M. Bates (Aust) 6–4, 6–3
N. Y. Mandelstam (URS) d. A. Kollontai (URS) 7–5, 6–4
A. Pauker (Rom) d. **(10)C. G. Chanel (Fra)** 4–6, 6–4, 6–3
(2)S. de Beauvoir (Fra) d. R. Draper (USA) 6–4, 5–7, 6–4

ROUND FOUR

C. E. Stead (Aust) d. R. Luxemburg (Pol) (forfeit)
B. Smith (USA) d. M. Elliott (USA) 6–3, 3–6, 6–3
J. Rhys (Dom) d. **(6)G. Stein (USA)** 7–5, 6–4
E. St. V. Millay (USA) d. **(3)A. Pavlova (URS)** 5–7, 6–3, 7–5
(4)S. Bernhardt (Fra) d. F. Hodgkins (NZ) 3–6, 6–3, 6–4
(15)A. A. G. Akhmatova (URS) d. **(7)A. V. Stephen-Woolf (Eng)** 4–6, 6–3, 6–4
H. Arendt (Ger) d. N. Y. Mandelstam (URS) 6–4, 5–7, 6–2
(2)S. de Beauvoir (Fra) d. A. Pauker (Rom) 2–6, 6–3, 7–5

QUARTERFINALS

B. Smith (USA) d. C. E. Stead (Aust) 3–6, 6–4, 6–2
E. St. V. Millay (USA) d. J. Rhys (Dom) 6–2, 3–6, 6–4
(15)A. A. G. Akhmatova (URS) d. **(4)S. Bernhardt (Fra)** 1–6, 6–4, 6–2
H. Arendt (Ger) d. **(2)S. de Beauvoir (Fra)** 6–4, 7–5

SEMIFINALS

E. St. V. Millay (USA) d. B. Smith (USA) (forfeit)
(15)A. A. G. Akhmatova (URS) d. H. Arendt (Ger) 1–6, 6–4, 7–5

FINAL

(15)A. A. G. Akhmatova (URS) d. E. St. V. Millay (USA) 5–7, 6–4, 19–17

MEN'S DOUBLES

ROUND ONE

(1)Sartre and Camus d. Eluard and Prevert 6–4, 6–2, 3–6, 7–5
(9)Magritte and Dali d. Gershwin and Gershwin 4–6, 6–1, 7–5, 6–3
Leavis and Lawrence d. Benjamin and Scholem 6–3, 6–4, 6–2
(5)Chaplin and O'Neill d. Caruso and Toscanini 6–2, 5–7, 6–4, 6–4
Shostakovich and Prokofiev d. **(6)Brecht and Weill** 6–2, 6–1, 6–4
(10)Cocteau and Picasso d. Milne and Disney 6–2, 6–1, 6–3
Wodehouse and Isherwood d. **(15)Chesterton and Belloc** 7–5, 6–2, 6–2
(3)Chekhov and Miller d. Lardner and Fitzgerald 6–2, 6–4, 7–5
Benchley and Thurber d. **(4)Einstein and Gödel** 7–5, 6–3, 4–6, 3–6, 6–2
Chandler and Hammett d. **(14)Gropius and Le Corbusier** 6–1, 6–4, 4–6, 6–4
(11)Kafka and Muir d. Arlen and Carmichael 6–4, 1–6, 3–6, 6–3, 6–2
(7)Auden and MacNeice d. Rutherford and Bohr 1–6, 6–3, 6–4, 6–4
Hope and Crosby d. **(8)Bakst and Blok** 6–4, 4–6, 6–3, 6–4
(13)Braque and Derain d. Léger and Keaton 6–1, 3–6, 7–5, 6–3
Runyon and Low d. **(12)Marx and Eliot** 6–1, 4–6, 6–0, 6–2
(2)Beckett and Duchamp d. Jung and Jung 6–4, 6–4, 6–2

ROUND TWO

(9)Magritte and Dali d. **(1)Sartre and Camus** 6–2, 7–5, 6–3
(5)Chaplin and O'Neill d. Leavis and Lawrence 6–3, 6–2, 6–4
(10)Cocteau and Picasso d. Shostakovich and Prokofiev 6–4, 4–6, 7–5, 6–2
(3)Chekhov and Miller d. Wodehouse and Isherwood 6–2, 5–7, 6–4, 6–3
Chandler and Hammett d. Benchley and Thurber 3–6, 4–6, 7–5, 7–5, 6–4
(7)Auden and MacNeice d. **(11)Kafka and Muir** 6–2, 6–4, 6–3
(13)Braque and Derain d. Hope and Crosby 7–5, 6–3, 6–1
(2)Beckett and Duchamp d. Runyon and Low 5–7, 7–5, 5–7, 7–5, 7–5

QUARTERFINALS

(9)Magritte and Dali d. **(5)Chaplin and O'Neill** 2–6, 6–4, 6–2, 6–1
(3)Chekhov and Miller d. **(10)Cocteau and Picasso** 5–7, 6–4, 6–3, 6–2
Chandler and Hammett d. **(7)Auden and MacNeice** 2–6, 6–4, 6–2, 6–3
(2)Beckett and Duchamp d. **(13)Braque and Derain** 6–4, 7–6, 5–7, 6–3

SEMIFINALS

(9)Magritte and Dali d. **(3)Chekhov and Miller** 3–6, 6–4, 6–3, 6–4
(2)Beckett and Duchamp d. Chandler and Hammett 4–6, 6–4, 6–2, 7–5

FINAL

(2)Beckett and Duchamp d. **(9)Magritte and Dali** 1–6, 2–6, 7–5, 7–5, 10–8

WOMEN'S DOUBLES

ROUND ONE

(1)Earhart and Cather d. West and Nin 6–2, 1–6, 7–5
Lenya and Dietrich d. **(16)Roosevelt and Luce** 7–6, 6–4
Kulthum and Sh'arawi d. **(15)Christie and Sayers** 6–2, 4–6, 6–4
Gonne-MacBride and Markievicz d. **(7)Blyton and Potter** 6–4, 6–2
(6)Sackville-West and Stephen-Woolf d. Fontanne and Nazimova 6–2, 7–5
Prichard and Richardson d. **(14)Parker and Ferber** 7–6, 5–7, 9–7
Draper and Elliott d. **(13)Bishop and McCarthy** 6–4, 1–6, 7–5
(3)Riefenstahl and Hari d. Mead and Stark 6–1, 3–6, 6–3
(4)Stein and Toklas d. Brice and Lillie 6–2, 6–3
(12)Mansfield and Hodgkins d. O'Keeffe and Kahlo 3–6, 6–4, 6–4
Naidu and Pandit d. **(10)Schiaparelli and Chanel** 6–3, 6–3
(5)de Valois and Pavlova d. Rubenstein and Arden 6–2, 6–1
Baker and Smith d. **(8)Duncan and Graham** (forfeit)
(9)Akhmatova and Arendt d. Campbell and Thorndike 4–6, 6–1, 6–0
(11)Keller and Sullivan d. Bankhead and Bara 6–4, 2–6, 6–2
Stern and Mandelstam d. **(2)Beach and Monier** 7–5, 7–5

ROUND TWO

Lenya and Dietrich d. **(1)Earhart and Cather** 6–3, 6–4
Gonne-MacBride and Markievicz d. Kulthum and Sh'arawi 6–3, 4–6, 7–5
(6)Sackville-West and Stephen–Woolf d. Prichard and Richardson 4–6, 6–3, 6–2
Draper and Elliott d. **(3)Riefenstahl and Hari** 6–1, 6–2
(12)Mansfield and Hodgkins d. **(4)Stein and Toklas** 6–3, 2–6, 6–4
(5)de Valois and Pavlova d. Naidu and Pandit 7–5, 6–3
(9)Akhmatova and Arendt d. Baker and Smith (forfeit)
(11)Keller and Sullivan d. Stern and Mandelstam (forfeit)

QUARTERFINALS

Lenya and Dietrich d. Gonne-MacBride and Markievicz 6–3, 2–6, 6–4
(6)**Sackville–West and Stephen–Woolf** d. Draper and Elliott 1–6, 6–4, 7–5
(12)**Mansfield and Hodgkins** d. (5)**de Valois and Pavlova** 5–7, 7–5, 6–3
(11)**Keller and Sullivan** d. (9)**Akhmatova and Arendt** 6–4, 7–5

SEMIFINALS

(12)**Mansfield and Hodgkins** d. (11)**Keller and Sullivan** 7–5, 6–3
Lenya and Dietrich d. (6)**Sackville-West and Stephen-Woolf** 6–4, 5–7, 6–3

FINAL

(12)**Mansfield and Hodgkins** d. Lenya and Dietrich 2–6, 6–4, 6–4

MIXED DOUBLES

ROUND ONE

(1)**Sartre and de Beauvoir** d. Weill and Lenya 6–3, 6–2
Wilding and Elliott d. (9)**Heidegger and Arendt** 6–1, 6–2
(16)**Keynes and Lopokova** d. Disney and Potter 6–1, 6–0
(5)**Astaire and Rogers** d. Tolkien and Blyton 6–1, 6–3
(6)**Freud and Klein** d. Hitler and Riefenstahl 6–2, 6–3
Leacock and Lillie d. (10)**Steegmuller and O'Keeffe** 7–5, 2–6, 6–1
Beckett and Guggenheim d. (15)**Stein and Toklas** 6–4, 6–4
(4)**Mandelstam and Mandelstam** d. Strachey and Stephen-Woolf 7–5, 6–4
(3)**Shaw and Campbell** d. Liebnecht and Luxemburg (forfeit)
St. V. Millay and partner d. (8)**Moore and Hepworth** 6–3, 6–2
Fields and West d. (7)**Rivera and Kahlo** 7–5, 6–0
Lawrence and Mansfield d. (13)**Stanislavsky and Nazimova** 7–5, 6–3
Chandler and Rhys d. (14)**Tracy and Hepburn** 6–2, 6–3
Rahv and McCarthy d. (11)**Wells and West** 6–2, 6–3
Bankhead and partner d. (12)**Hammett and Hellman** 6–3, 6–3
(2)**Nijinsky and Pavlova** d. Benchley and Parker 7–5, 7–5

ROUND TWO

Wilding and Elliott d. (1)**Sartre and de Beauvoir** 6–3, 6–3
(5)**Astaire and Rogers** d. (16)**Keynes and Lopokova** 6–2, 6–4
(6)**Freud and Klein** d. Leacock and Lillie 7–5, 6–3
Beckett and Guggenheim d. (4)**Mandelstam and Mandelstam** (forfeit)

(3)Shaw and Campbell d. St. V. Millay and partner 6–2, 6–3
Lawrence and Mansfield d. Fields and West 6–2, 6–4
Rahv and McCarthy d. Chandler and Rhys 4–6, 7–5, 6–2
Bankhead and partner d. **(2)Nijinsky and Pavlova** (forfeit)

QUARTERFINALS

(5)Astaire and Rogers d. Wilding and Elliott 2–6, 6–3, 6–4
(6)Freud and Klein d. Beckett and Guggenheim 6–2, 6–4
Lawrence and Mansfield d. **(3)Shaw and Campbell** 6–3, 5–7, 6–3
Bankhead and partner d. Rahv and McCarthy 4–6, 6–3, 6–2

SEMIFINALS

(6)Freud and Klein d. **(5)Astaire and Rogers** 7–5, 6–4
Bankhead and partner d. Lawrence and Mansfield 3–6, 6–2, 6–4

FINAL

Bankhead and partner d. **(6)Freud and Klein** 6–3, 6–4